SEX TOY TRICKS

SEX TOY TRICKS

More Than 125 Ways to Accessorize Good Sex

by Jay Wiseman

Greenery
Press

Published in the United States by Greenery Press, 3739 Balboa Ave. #195, San Francisco, CA 94121.

Special thanks from the publishers to Diana & alexi from Texas for their invaluable assistance in making this book a reality.

ISBN #0-9639763-4-6

Table of Contents

Acknowledgements
(The "Thank You" List)

It's been a distinct privilege to talk with the various people listed below. I feel very honored that they would judge me trustworthy enough to share such very personal experiences and knowledge. I hope I have done justice to what they shared. My grateful thanks to all.

Ann Marie	Kim Airs
Annye and Christophe	Leona Joy
Anonymous	Libby Donahue
Cecilia Tan	Lynn Craig
Charles Moser	Maggi Rubenstein
China	Maryann
Dell Williams	Merrill Seldes
Don't tell them where you got that	Mic Bergen
Dossie Easton	Moriah St. Cyr
Francesca Guido	Ms. Margo
Glenna	Nightlace
Helen Wolfe	Oberon and Morning Glory Zell
Jaymes Easton	Tedde Rinker-Davis
Jennifer Thompson	Trish
Joan Levine	Verdant
John Warren	Wally Daniels
Karen Kummerfeldt	Wilhelmina Moosepunch
Karen Mendelsohn	

Additional Thanks

Staff members of the following stores also graciously contributed material. If you call, please mention this book.

Note: The stores listed below are something of a mixed lot. Most are retail, walk-in stores, but some are mail-order-only operations. Some offer merchandise and books, and some only offer books. Some offer classes and workshops.

Blowfish San Francisco, CA (415) 864-0880
Camouflage Santa Cruz, CA (408) 423-7613
Circlet Press P.O. Box 15143 Boston, MA
Come Again New York, NY (212) 308-9394
Diversified Services Boston, MA (617) 787-7426
Eve's Garden New York, NY (212) 757-8651
Good Vibrations San Francisco, CA (415) 974-8989
Grand Opening Boston, MA (617) 731-2626
Love Season Lynnewood, WA (206) 775-4502
Passion Flower Oakland, CA (510) 601-7750
Pleasure Chest Philadelphia, PA (215) 561-7480
QSM San Francisco, CA (415) 550-7776
Taboo Tabou Chicago, IL (312) 548-2266
The Noose New York, NY (212) 807-1789
Toys In Babeland Seattle, WA (206) 328-2914
Xandria Brisbane, CA (800) 242-2823

If you'd like for your store to be listed in future printings, feel free to contact us with some Tricks of your own.

Finally, once again, my deepest thanks to Janet. Thank you for five wonderful, deeply loving, years together – with (please, God) more to come! Thank you for being one of the most brilliant, insightful, creative, and sex-positive women that ever existed. Thank you for your many contributions to helping make this book a reality.

Finally, and a bit humbly, thank you for your world-class patience with me during the final stages of this book's creation. I love you absolutely, unconditionally, and with all my heart, just the way you are.

April 28, 1995 San Francisco, CA.

Warning and Disclaimer

Being sexual with the right person, in the right way, at the right time, in the right location, and for the right reasons can be an incredibly positive experience for everyone involved. If any of the above is not right, however, then problems can emerge.

Erotic energy is one of the most powerful forces in our world. Respect and pay attention to that power and you can experience bliss. Disrespect or ignore that power and you might not live to regret it.

The primary purpose of "Sex Toy Tricks" is to provide information and advice that will help make good sex between informed, consenting adults a little bit better. It also provides basic information to help people understand their situations, make them aware of possible alternatives, cope with problems, and find helpful resources.

Please do not think of this book as any kind of medical, legal, psychological, or other professional advice. It most certainly is not intended as a substitute for proper sex therapy. Most of its core information, particularly the "Tricks" themselves, was discovered on my own, taught to me by lovers I have had, shared with me by friends during highly informal conversations (many has been the time since the first "Tricks" book was published that someone has come up to me and said "I've got a Trick for you"), or sent to me either in the mail or over the internet. Please keep that in mind when considering this book's contents.

Almost without question, there are at least a few factual errors in this book, and probably a few typographical errors as well. Also, it's very common, in this and many other fields, that information believed to be accurate at the time of publication is later revealed to be inaccurate – sometimes only slightly so, sometimes very much so. If you have even the slightest question about the accuracy or safety of anything in here, please check with independent sources. If their recommendations differ from mine, please let me know. By the way, please remember that not all professional advice is equally complete, accurate, up to date, and unbiased. By all means get an independent "second opinion" (and maybe even a "third opinion") if you feel even the slightest need for it.

Feedback Please!

If you think you have found a factual error, typographical error, or other inaccuracy or omission in this book, please let me know so that this can be corrected in future printings.

No one associated with writing, editing, printing, distributing, or selling this book, or in any other way associated with it, is in any way liable for any damages that result from acting on the information herein. While I have most certainly not put anything in here that I consider likely to be harmful, understand clearly that you act on the information in this book entirely at your own risk.

Why Am I Writing This Book?

The Scope of This Book

Well, folks, the saga of the "Tricks" books continues to grow. As some of you know, I had a "Tricks" article appear in the December, 1994 issue of Playboy (the one with Bo Derek's face on the cover). People continue to send me Tricks in the mail, or over the internet (I'm jaybob@crl.com), or to tell me about them in person. I must confess that I never expected such an overwhelming reaction.

That I should be writing this particular book is also more than slightly surprising to me. (Was it John Lennon who said "Life is what happens while you're making other plans?") In 1994, it dawned on me that I had a logical gap in my line of sexuality books. I had my "Tricks" books, which involved mainly the bodies of the people involved (and a few household items), and I had "SM 101: A Realistic Introduction" to tell people the basics of how to use SM equipment, but I didn't have a book that dealt with ordinary sex toys. Thus was born the idea for this book.

This book deals with how to use items that were manufactured and purchased specifically for relatively "vanilla" sexual activity. It will not deal extensively with SM-type activities and/or equipment – although it will cover some basic SM safety info.

Assumptions

In presenting the material in this book, I am making the following assumptions about your situation. If any of these assumptions are not true in your case, please modify your behavior accordingly.

I'm assuming:

1. That both of you are willing (and, hopefully, eager) to have sex with each other. Consent is absolutely essential.

2. That being sexual with each other will not violate any agreements you have made with others about your sexual behavior.

3. That both of you reasonably understand what you are doing. Having sex with someone too young, senile, feeble-minded, intoxicated, unconscious, or otherwise unable to understand and consent to what is happening may get you charged with rape, even if no force was used. If they're too drunk to drive, they're probably too drunk to have sex.

4. That both of you have reached the age of consent in your state (and that you live in the United States). I believe the age of consent is as low as twelve in a few states and as high as eighteen in many others. An act that is perfectly legal on one side of a state line may cost you a lengthy prison sentence if done on the other side of it. Make sure you know the age of consent in your state.

   Your local library should have a copy of your state's criminal code in its reference section. Reading its sections on rape, incest, indecent exposure, lewd and lascivious behavior, assault, contributing to the deliquency of a minor, and related sections may be very instructive. Asking a local attorney or police officer (that you already know well) can also help, but remember that opinions, knowledge, and objectivity can vary widely, even among such "experts." Try to get information from more than one source.

   (By the way, sex between blood relatives may be illegal no matter what the age of those involved. If you cannot legally marry a particular person, it may also be illegal for you to have sex with each other. This could be true even if both of you are over 18 and both fully consent.)

5. That the acts I'm describing are legal in your state. Although the laws are rarely enforced, oral sex, anal intercourse, and other practices are still a crime in some states, even if done by consenting adults in private. (Possession of some sorts of sex toys is against the law in some areas.) Find out your state's laws and, where appropriate, work to change them. This whole area is badly in need of legislative reform.

6. That no risk of passing on a sexually transmitted disease exists. These days, that's a *big* assumption. If such a risk does exist, please modify what you do. If you have herpes or if you have tested positive for the HIV virus and have sex with someone without first telling them about that, you could be arrested. If your partner becomes infected, you could also be sued. If you have any questions, one information source is the National Sexually Transmitted Disease Hotline at (800) 227-8922.

Criteria

For inclusion in this book, a Trick usually had to meet the following criteria:

1. It had to be something that could be done pretty much on impulse in the here and now. Nothing too elaborate.

2. It had to involve equipment purchased specifically for the purpose of erotic enjoyment – not ordinary household goods (that's "Supermarket Tricks"), but items intended only for sexual use.

3. It had to be safe. I included nothing I thought likely to endanger people.

4. It had to pertain directly to sex or to a very closely related matter.

5. It had to have a successful track record. I looked for Tricks that had consistently made more than one lover gasp, sigh, and moan.

6. It had to appeal to a wide, mainstream audience. The Trick couldn't be too far out or kinky. (Again, that's another book.) Most of the Tricks therefore involve masturbation, fellatio, cunnilingus, vaginal penetration, and anal penetration.

Selection, Balance, and Orientation

The Tricks in this book are largely a reflection of the material I received. I interviewed dozens of sex toy fans, male and female, gay, straight, and bisexual, to come up with the Tricks you see here.

I've tried to present as many Tricks as possible in a "gender neutral" manner. In most cases, it doesn't matter whether the people involved are straight or gay.

Please remember that I publish a series of "Tricks" books. If you feel a certain category is under-represented, by all means send in material to balance things out.

I deliberately included many masturbation Tricks in this book as my own way of encouraging safer sex.

I decided to, for the most part, leave out material regarding SM, bisexuality, swinging, tantra, multiple-partner sex, and so forth. Those are specialized areas, and their practices and customs are far too extensive to describe properly in this book. I did include contact information if you're interested in exploring them further. You may also find useful information in some of my other books (listed on the last page).

The Limits Of Tricks

You know, and I know, that lovemaking should not be reduced to Tricks. Tricks are to erotic play what spices are to food. A few carefully chosen ones make the experience more intense and pleasurable. Too many spoil things.

It's entirely possible to have a wonderful and completely satisfying sex life without knowing the Tricks in this book, or any others. Good sex is based on caring about your partner's well-being, really wanting to have sex with them (and, of course them really wanting to have sex with you), and observing the responsibilities that go along with that. Still, adding a carefully chosen spice now and then helps things along.

Key Point: Your underlying feelings towards the other person, and theirs toward you, greatly affect whether or not a Trick will improve your erotic play. As one lady told me, "If I really like him, then he almost can't do anything wrong. If I really don't like him, then he can't even breathe right."

When a Trick Bombs

Each person has their own unique physical and emotional pattern of erotic responsiveness. Every now and then a Trick that always worked well before may utterly turn off a new partner. The key phrase for handling this situation is "show compassion for everyone involved, including yourself."

If what you did *really* turned your partner off, try not to take it personally. (You wouldn't be human if you didn't take it somewhat personally, but don't buy into that too deeply.) Remember, each person has their own pattern, and you can never completely know that pattern. Give them a brief apology, if that seems appropriate, then move on to something else. Little will be gained by debating the point, particularly right then. Save discussions for later.

On the other hand, if your partner starts to do something that really doesn't work for you, diplomatically let them know that as soon as you can. Being "polite" in this situation will only allow your displeasure to build to uncontrollable levels. Speak up (politely, please) as soon as possible. Remember, this is almost undoubtedly not willful misconduct on their part. They are probably doing it in an attempt, however misguided, to arouse you. Speak up – but give them the benefit of the doubt, especially if this partner is relatively new.

Find Their Envelope

Each person has their own erotic response pattern, something I've come to think of as their "envelope." One of your main tasks as a good lover is to find your partner's envelope. Something that is wildly erotic for one person can be grossly unpleasant, and even traumatic, for another.

The envelope varies widely from person to person. It also varies over time with the same person. Find their envelope before you try too many Tricks, and remember that the location and content of that envelope change over time.

Intoxicants

Provided you don't have a substance abuse problem, light use of intoxicants can do a lot to enhance your mood. They can relax tense muscles, take your mind off the worries of the day, and generally calm you down and bring you into the here and now.

I prefer wine. Beer tends to fill up my bladder too quickly (and too often). Harder liquors take me more out of it than I like. I quit using recreational drugs of any kind many years ago.

More than light intoxicant use is asking for trouble. Your judgment becomes dangerously cloudy. Your coordination suffers. You may become too out of it to be sexual at all.

AIDS prevention experts are campaigning against combining sex and intoxicants. They have found that many unsafe sex acts occur when, and – more importantly – only when, the people involved are intoxicated. They compare driving under the influence (D.U.I.) with having sex under the influence (S.U.I.) in terms of danger.

Remember that getting someone too drunk or stoned to understand what is happening and then having sex with them is rape.

If someone is so drunk or stoned that it would be a crime for them to drive, then it would also probably be a crime to have sex with them.

Sex and the Internet

In the last few years, the international computer network known as the Internet has skyrocketed in usage – particularly its sexuality-related areas.

Some places on the Internet, devoted to the discussion of specific subjects, are called newsgroups. There, people can read and place messages related to the topic. Several thousand newsgroups exist and about 100 new ones appear each month. In addition, thousands of pages on the World Wide Web are devoted to sexuality issues – search engines such as Yahoo can help you find them. If you're interested in aviation, bicycling, stamp collecting, MTV, or virtually any other subject, you can find an international network of kindred spirits on the net.

More than a dozen newsgroups are devoted to various aspects of sexuality. Most are called "alt" (for alternative) groups. Some of the best-known are:

alt.sex	alt.sex.masturbation
alt.sex.bondage	alt.polyamory
alt.sex.swingers	alt.sexual.abuse.recovery
alt.sex.anal	alt.transgendered
alt.sex.enemas	alt.politics.sex
alt.sex.safe	alt.recovery.sexual.addiction
alt.sex.stories	alt.sex.wizards

In addition, at least two newsgroups exist for the sole purpose of marketing sex-related goods. Check out alt.sex.marketplace and alt.sex.erotica.marketplace (the busier of the two) for more information. I can be reached as jaybob@crl.com on the net.

Where To Buy Sex Toys

I've got to write this chapter carefully, because I can visualize all my vendors jumping up and down shouting "From me! From me!" I do suggest that you give your business to a local resource if possible.

There are three major sources of toys: walk-in retail stores, mail-order vendors, and pleasure parties. Let's look at each.

How to Find Walk-in Sex Toy Vendors in Your Local Community

Open your yellow pages to "Lingerie Dealers, Retail" and begin your search there. Then turn to "Bookstores," "Leather," and "Videos." In addition to traditional adult bookstores, we now have a growing number of "sex-positive" erotic boutiques and leather stores. If you can, visit several different stores before making purchases. (Most are open on weekends, so spending the day touring them with your partner can make for a wonderful "erotic holiday.")

Different stores cater to different clienteles. Most traditional adult bookstores are aimed at heterosexual men. Some stores attract a mostly gay male clientele. Some are aimed primarily at women. You may be treated in subtly (or not so subtly!) different ways at different stores. Try to give your business to a store in which you feel comfortable.

A Caution for Straight Men

One caution that I'll give to my straight male readers: you might think it would be a great idea to try to hang out in the women-oriented stores trying to meet partners. I can just hear some of you thinking, "Hey, *lots* of babes go into places like that, and they're already horny. This will be almost too easy."

The truth is that a woman, especially if she is by herself, may be hyper-nervous about being in such a store. Any pick-up attempts, no matter how "innocent and friendly," may send her bolting for the door, perhaps never to return – and that's tragic. Such behavior has a *very* good chance of getting you kicked out, and perhaps permanently banned. Trying to pick up women in an erotic boutique is just not a good idea. Don't do it. (The clerks don't let other women hit on their female customers, either.)

Guys, if you want to go to a woman-oriented erotic boutique to buy toys, books, and so forth, by all means go. They'd love your business. Just understand that these places have had to deal with a lot of male jerks, so they may act slightly wary towards you. When I go into such a store, I always keep my distance from the women customers, and I wouldn't dream of speaking to one of them unless she spoke to me first.

It's fine to ask the female clerks questions about the literature or equipment, and they should be happy to make recommendations. Just don't get too explicit. They're not getting paid to "talk sexy" with you – and they have to deal with such nonsense entirely too often.

As a subpoint, it's fine to call on the phone and ask about store hours, location, and so forth. Just keep your conversation businesslike and brief. Asking her to "describe every item in the store and tell me how to use it" will likely get you little except a dial tone (or a curt and businesslike suggestion that you buy and read this very book).

A Few Suggestions for the Nervous Woman

Many women report major, positive changes in their lives, and not just their sex lives, after reading literature or using equipment they bought in an erotic boutique. Indeed, sometimes just going into one can be a revealing, educational experience. More and more erotic boutiques go out of their way to make female customers comfortable. Please don't let your fears become so strong that you never go.

Here are a few hints about how to gather your courage.

1. **Going in is not really all that risky.**
   You are not likely to be approached by horny, crude male (or female) customers. The staff, like the staff of any store, would probably be quite happy if you bought something. They have no reason to make you feel uncomfortable, and many reasons to make you feel comfortable. It's very common to have a "hey, that was fun!" feeling after a first visit.

2. **Go with friends, particularly female friends.**
   There is courage in numbers. You can lend each other emotional support, and the visit can become a delicious subject for later conversations. Remember, you don't have to buy something with all of your friends looking on; you can come back later by yourself. Also, many stores sell by mail order, so you can look over the merchandise and quietly snag a mail-order catalog, or call the store later and ask them to send you one.

3. **Go with one close friend or your primary partner.**
   You almost undoubtedly won't need someone to "protect" you during your visit to an erotic boutique, but going with someone can provide some reassurance. Just make sure it's someone with whom you feel comfortable talking about the store's merchandise.

4. **Go at a time when the store is not very busy.**
   Erotic boutiques tend to be busier on weekends than during the week. During the week, they are often busier in the late afternoon and early evening, when people get off work, than earlier during the day. They are also busier than usual before Christmas and Valentine's Day.

5. **Go to a store in another town.**
   While I still feel it's best to buy locally if you can, sometimes it's prudent to wait until you're in another city, where

nobody is likely to know you – especially if you're well known in your local community. (When, oh when, will we begin to regard sexuality as just another part of life? We don't have these concerns regarding visits to a grocery or hardware store.) Many people take advantage of a trip to cities like New York or San Francisco to "sneak in" a visit to an erotic boutique.

6. Above all else, go.
    Whatever strategy you adopt, an actual visit to an erotic boutique can be a moving experience that can teach you a lot about yourself, sexuality, and other aspects of life. If you're interested in a visit, please don't let your fears cheat you.

Mail-Order Businesses

Several companies do a first-rate job of providing information and equipment by mail order. They're not hard to find. (After all, *they're* trying to find *you*.) Many run ads in periodicals that deal with sexuality, relationships, and/or health issues. Magazines aimed specifically at a male or at a female audience often contain such ads, usually toward the back. Mail-order companies also advertise on the internet's alt.sex.marketplace and alt.sex.erotica.marketplace newsgroups, as well as on the World Wide Web.

These companies may want a few dollars, which they will usually credit towards your first order, in exchange for their catalogs. These catalogs often contain a lot of information, and allow you to comparison shop. I suggest you acquire at least three.

Pleasure Parties

These events, usually all-female but occasionally for couples, in many ways resemble "Tupperware parties" except that the goods being sold probably won't end up in your refrigerator or pantry. Typically, a woman hosts such a party in her home and invites several female friends. The (female) sales rep displays the various items and provides information on their use. Orders for goods are often taken in private and may be fullfilled either at the event or by later delivery. These events are often both highly educational and a great deal of fun. To learn more, check your phone book under "Party Planning."

In summary, you have several effective options for buying sex toys. Do some comparing and find the one that feels most comfortable to you.

A Tour of an Erotic Boutique

Let's take a look around a "typical" erotic boutique. These have come into being since the sexual revolution of the late Sixties and early Seventies. Most are owned/managed/staffed by women, and have a distinctly woman-oriented style. These stores almost always welcome men provided the guys keep in mind what the female staff and customers are there for – and *not* there for.

The stores contain a wide variety of merchandise. Indeed, a few are so jammed that it can be a bit difficult to move around in them. They will usually stock a variety of books (including such timeless classics as "Tricks," "SM 101," and "The Sexually Dominant Woman") and a number of sexuality-related magazines.

Many also carry videos, lingerie, jewelry (keep your eyes open for the "clit clip" and the "tit-a-lizer"), erotic board games, novelty items, lubricants, SM gear, and, of course, a wide variety of condoms, gloves, and other safer sex supplies.

And then there are the toys, all those marvelous toys – and so many different types of them! Let's look at the major categories and cover some of the basic points.

Vibrators

Some people get nervous about the idea of using a vibrator or other sex toy. Please trust me when I say that they're not addictive and that they'll never replace a cuddly partner. (They can be a wonderful supplement, however, for both of you.) There are two general categories of vibrators – plug-in and battery-powered – and many different subtypes of each.

The only vibrator problem reported with any noticeable frequency is that sometimes prolonged exposure to the stronger sensations produced by some vibrators can make the stimulated area temporarily less sensitive to more subtle forms of stimulation, or even to the vibration itself. This is called "numbing out" and goes away within half an hour or so. With vibrators, as with other sex toys, part of your learning and exploration involve discovering what's "too little," what's "too much," and what's "just right" (ahhhhhhh) for you. Relax, explore, and enjoy.

Plug-In Vibrators

Plug-in vibrators, as a rule, provide stronger, more spread-out vibrations than battery-operated vibrators provide. However, their electrical motors also give off considerably more heat. (If you run an plug-in vibrator long enough, it can become too hot to touch to bare skin. Prolonged usage can also damage the motor. Be sure to read, and save, the directions.) Most such vibrators come with two different speed settings. Most also come with a cord at least six feet long, but you'll probably find it a good idea to purchase an extension cord. (It's also possible to buy an adapter called the Humdinger 2 that goes between the plug and the wall socket and turns the vibrator's steady, constant buzz into a variable-speed pulsation.)

Plug-in vibrators come in two general subcategories: wand-type and coil-type. Both types have many loyal fans.

Wand-Type Plug-In Vibrators. Most wand-type vibrators have a vibrating head that attaches by a narrow, flexible neck to a long, cylindrical handle. (There's even a two-headed version!) Wand-type vibrators come very highly recommended. While I hesitate to make specific recommendations, the Hitachi Magic Wand is definitely worth checking out. (I recently bought one to give as a present.) It's also possible to buy attachments, such as a g-spot stimulator, to fit over the wand's head.

A wand-type rechargeable vibrator is on the market and well regarded. Users state that its vibrations are almost as strong as those from a regular wand, and they like its cordlessness. A single charge usually lasts forty minutes or so.

Coil-Type Plug-In Vibrators. Most coil-type vibrators are smaller than the wand-types, and have a handle on one end – kind of like a hairbrush. A small post protrudes from the bottom of the main section, and attachments go there. Coil-type vibrators usually have a more focused vibration and typically cost slightly less than wand-type vibrators. As a rule, coil-types tend to be quieter than wand-types. The store should let you turn on a few different types to check this. Coil-types also come with a wide variety of attachments. (An adapter is available to also make these attachments usable on wand-type vibrators.) One of my past lovers made a point of gleefully trying out every single attachment that came with my coil-type vibrator.

A unique sub-variety of coil-type vibrator is the "Swedish Massager," worn on the back of the hand to allow skin-to-skin contact.

When cleaning both wand and coil types of vibrators, be sure cleaning fluid doesn't get into the motor section. Wipe the exterior with a moistened cloth and allow to dry. The attachments (but not the vibrators themselves!) are "dunkable" and can even be run through the dishwasher.

One caution: Some wand-type vibrators (which are usually sold in more conventional stores) have the capacity to give off "deep heat" if you throw a specific switch. I have heard reports of severe burns from using this feature during genital play. Obviously, this is not a recommended practice.

Battery-Operated Vibrators

Many, many different varieties of battery-operated vibrators exist. The "standard" seven-inch by one-inch plastic vibrator is probably the most widely used sex toy in the world.

Battery-operated vibrators are relatively inexpensive, highly portable, and widely available. Their vibration tends to be less strong than that of a plug-in vibrator. They range from thumb-sized to more than a foot long. Battery-operated vibrators come in both single-speed and multiple speed versions. They are made of plastic, soft vinyl, latex, and other materials. Those made from a special soft synthetic compound are called "jellies."

Battery-operated vibrators come in many, many different sizes and shapes. The major types include:

- Standard, penis-shaped vibrators ranging in length from four inches to nearly a foot long and from less than one inch to more than two inches in diameter.

- Vibrators flared at the base with small bumps or beads contained within the vibrator to give additional stimulation to the outer portion of the vaginal canal (where most of her nerves are).

- Mostly straight vibrators that curve at the end to use for G-spot stimulation.

- "Butterfly" vibrators that lie over the woman's vulva and attach to her body by two straps.

- "Over and Under" vibrators that consist of a vibrator for internal stimulation and a separate clitoral stimulator on top, with a separate, variable speed control for each function. (These also have something of a cult following.)

- There is one particular type of battery-operated vibrator that I suggest you make a point of checking out. It goes by various names including the "bullet" and the "pearl." It's a very small, relatively inexpensive, cylinder-shaped vibrator – only two inches long and less than an inch in diameter – with a cord leading to its battery pack. This small size allows it to get into a number of places that a larger vibrator just can't go. (To use it for anal insertion, see Trick 116.) A number of stores recommend this particular model as a "first vibrator."

Ben Wa Balls

These are two balls inserted into the vagina. The smaller ones are all metal and not joined together. The larger ones (Duotone) contain a metal ball within a plastic ball, with the movement of the small ball inside the larger creating the sensations, and are joined by a loop of string. Like the bullet, you should take precautions if you're using ben wa balls for anal insertion.

Many women report that the sensation of ben wa balls alone is too subtle for them. However, those who love them really do love them – and many of those who don't are converted by using them in concert with other sex toys and activities. (For example, some women can wear the small metal ones during intercourse.)

Cock Rings

The arteries that carry blood into the penis are located deep within it and the veins that carry blood out of the penis are located closer to the surface. By applying a constricting band – usually around both the penis and the scrotum – an erection can often be made firmer and more long-lasting; how much so varies from man to man. This constricting band is commonly known as a cock ring.

Cock rings come in many different forms. They are made of leather, latex, steel, and other materials. Some encircle both the penis and scrotum, some encircle only the penis. Some come with stimulators for her vaginal/clitoral area. Some also wrap around the top of the scrotum and/or between the testicles (reminding me of that bra commercial advising how it "lifts and separates"). Some come with attachment points for bondage games. Some even come with a small vibrator attached.

For starters, I suggest that you buy a simple leather cock ring. They're inexpensive, highly adjustable, can be worn just around the scrotum, just around the penis, or around both penis and scrotum. Experiment to find the desired degree of tightness. A "too tight" cock ring can make orgasm painful, and even divert some to the semen up into the bladder. A "too loose" cock ring is of little value or interest. A "just right" cock ring is delightful for all concerned.

Dildoes

My dictionary defines a dildo as an artificial penis, although many folks uncomfortable with that implication prefer to define it as a device for penetrative sex. A dildo can be used for vaginal intercourse, anal intercourse, or fellatio play. Like vibrators, dildoes come in many different sizes, colors, and configurations. There are even double-headed models.

Dildoes are made of many different materials, including latex, rubber, "jelly," vinyl, leather, and silicone. Those flared at the base can be worn in a harness. (Adapters can be purchased that allow other dildoes to also be used this way.)

Many, many people, both men and women, love to be penetrated by a woman who is wearing a strap-on dildo. With the right partner and under the right circumstances, this can be an incredibly powerful experience for both people. Several different brands of harnesses are on the market, in a wide variety of configurations, materials, colors, and prices.

Silicone dildoes generally come highly recommended. They have distinctly life-like heft and flexibility, and they warm to body temperature quite nicely. However, they are noticeably more expensive than most other dildoes. Also, while they are reasonably sturdy, once a rip or tear starts in a silicone dildo there is usually little that can be done to save it. (Keep it away from various sharp points and abrasive surfaces – including the claws and teeth of family pets!) Some users report that silicone gets "floppy" after two or three years. I'm not sure I'd recommend a silicone dildo as a first purchase, but once you decide that you're "into" dildo play they're definitely worth a serious look. In particular, a double headed dildo called the "Animus Activator" (also sometimes called the boomerang) is worth a close look.

Butt Plugs

The anus and rectum are very erotic areas for many people. Some lucky folks can reach orgasm from anal stimulation alone. However, the rectum is a delicate area, and care must be taken not to damage it. Also, unlike the vagina, the rectum is not a closed-end system. Objects can and do get lost up into the rectum. (That complication is dealt with in a separate section of this book.) As a basic safety matter, toys intended for anal play should have some sort of device designed to prevent their being "inhaled" by the rectum. For most toys, this is a broad flare at their base.

Like vibrators and dildoes, butt plugs come in a variety of colors, sizes, and materials. It's important that a butt plug have a smooth surface, with no sharp seams or "rough spots." Trust me, such places will quickly become unpleasantly evident.

Butt plugs are slightly different than dildoes, and usually used differently. Plugs typically have a bulge slightly above the flared end, designed to keep the wearer from involuntarily pushing out the plug. Unlike dildoes, which are frequently thrust in and out in a manner similar to intercourse, butt plugs are usually inserted and left in place.

Anal beads are a form of "butt plug" worth special attention. They are a series of beads (various sizes are available) strung along a string. The beads are inserted one at a time into the rectum. Pulling them out, slowly or quickly according to taste, can create arousal or boost orgasm. Anal beads can be used during both self-play and partner play. One caution: Unfortunately, they often have a rough "seam" on them that could cause discomfort and even injury if removed too quickly. Be sure to inspect each bead and carefully file down any rough seams before you insert them.

SM Gear

Many stores now carry "formal" items of SM gear such as whips, restraints, and clamps. As you look these items over, please keep in mind that SM can potentially be extremely risky to your physical health, your emotional health, and the health of your relationship with your partner. To do SM safely, you'll need to get some "formal" training.

There are many excellent beginners' books on the market. Look for my own "SM 101: A Realistic Introduction." Also look for "The Sexually Dominant Woman: A Workbook for Nervous Beginners" by Lady Green, "The Loving Dominant" by John Warren, "Learning the Ropes" by Race Bannon, "Sensuous Magic" by Pat Califia, and "Screw the Roses, Send Me the Thorns," by Philip Miller and Molly Devon.

Most large cities now have clubs that offer lectures on how to engage in SM with adequate safety and consensuality. Feel free to ask the clerk about such clubs in your area. There are also several excellent discussion groups regarding this topic on the Internet, and informational sites on the World Wide Web.

SM is not just another form of sexuality. It has incredible potential, but it also has incredible risks. Both these facts require that you approach it in much the same way that you would approach something like scuba diving or mountain climbing. There is a lot to learn, and you need to go slowly at first.

Lubricants, Gels, Creams, and Lotions

Lubricants are almost more of a necessity than an accessory. They're a must for anal play, and often very useful for vaginal play. Older women often welcome some supplemental vaginal lubrication.

Advisory: When a vibrator is touched to skin, particularly one of the stronger vibrators, the rapid back-and-forth motion can sometimes actually abrade the area. "Vibrator burn" can be a real nuisance. Consider applying a layer of lubricant beforehand, particularly if you're using a strong vibrator on a sensitive body area. (Such lubrication can also make the sensation considerably more pleasant, even in the absence of problems.)

Different lubricants are meant for different purposes. Lubricants basically come in two general types: water-based and oil-based. The oil-based lubes, including most massage oils, tend to be a bit "heavier" and to stay slippery longer. Unfortunately, they break down latex products such as latex condoms and gloves. (Oil-based lubes can, however, be used with polyurethane products such as the Avanti condom and the Reality female condom.) Some women report yeast infections following the use of particular lubes; oil-based ones seem to cause more frequent problems. Water-based lubes are generally "lighter" and don't stay slippery as long, but this is easily fixed by adding a few drops of saliva or water. Flavored "lickable" lubricants are good for enhancing oral sex, particularly fellatio (a previous lover of mine relished the "hot cinnamon" flavor), but might be too sugary for penetration or cunnilingus.

Lubricants come with and without nonoxynol-9. This product is marketed as a spermicide and works well in that role. It also kills various microorganisms. Nonoxynol-9 may play a limited role in the prevention of sexually transmitted disease, but considerably more people than initially thought seem allergic to it, and its use has fallen somewhat out of favor. Possilbe alternatives include nonoxynol-15 and octoxynol-9.

Some lubricants contain local anesthetics such as lidocaine and benzocaine. These reportedly delay ejaculation and make anal intercourse easier. How useful they are in delaying ejaculation is debatable, and several authorities strongly recommend against their use in anal play. The rectum can be a delicate place. If some activity is causing pain, they feel you need to pay attention to this, not ignore it. Therefore, the use of lubricants containing a local anesthetic is not recommended for easing the difficulty of anal intercourse. (Use more lube instead.) There is a possible use for them in regard to oral sex, and this is covered in the "Tricks" section.

These are just a few of the major points regarding the more common toys. There's much more to learn. Feel free to browse in the store for a while, soaking your brain with knowledge.

A Few Don'ts Regarding Tricks

1. Don't spend too much time doing Tricks. It's far more important to stay in the here and now with your lover. Do a Trick "every now and then."

2. Don't try to do too many different Tricks in a single session. Again, that can distance you from your lover.

3. Don't be overly concerned with looking for opportunities to do a Trick. Let such opportunities appear naturally during the course of events. Men seem particularly vulnerable to this pitfall, thus giving rise to the somewhat bitter saying among many women, "There were three of us in bed: him, me, and his technique."

4. Never place anything in a woman's vagina if it's recently been in her (or, for that matter, any other person's) anus. Doing so can cause her to get an infection that will require a visit to a doctor and antibiotics to cure. For example, inserting your a dildo or your penis into her anus and then into her vagina would be very likely to cause such an infection. (A physician once told me that licking a woman's anus and then licking her vulva could cause her to get infected.) Anything used for anal play must first be thoroughly cleaned before it can be used for vaginal play.

5. Never seal your mouth over a woman's vagina and blow air into it. There are reports of women suffering fatal air embolisms from this practice. Menstruating women seem

to face a considerably higher-than-average risk. Such incidents are very, very rare, but they do happen.

6. Be careful about placing food items, especially sugary foods, in a woman's vagina. Many men and women recommended placing various foods in there and then eating them out (grapes had something of a cult following). These food can upset the vagina's natural pH balance and cause infections, particularly yeast infections. You can do such Tricks if you want, but if you do, then understand that you may have to deal with their effects "the morning after."

Egg Cream

The bullet- or egg-shaped vibrators are the smallest types. Tricksters report that inserting one *deep* into her vagina before intercourse can be great fun for both parties.

2

Sofa, So Good

While using a dildo on yourself can be very pleasurable, it can be limiting to have one hand occupied.
Try attaching the dildo to the leg of a couch or heavy chair, just a few inches above the floor. Then lie on your back, scoot yourself down "onto" it, and relax, with both hands now free for other activities.

3

Jingle Balls

Anal intercourse may be made more pleasurable for her (and thus for him, too) if she inserts a pair of ben wa balls into her vagina before being anally penetrated. The brass-within-plastic type has a particular following.

∴4∴
I Surrender

Insert an egg-type vibrator that has a long cord into your vagina, then hand the control box to your partner. Let them take charge of what sensations you feel, and when.

∴5∴
I'm Pickin' Up Good Vibrations

One way to make a vibrator less threatening to your partner is to offer to give them a massage with it. It feels wonderful to many folks on the tense muscles between the shoulder blades and across the mid-back, for example. If their feet are sore, try a vibrator foot massage. Trade off the vibrator with traditional massage hand strokes.

∴6∴
Sunny Side Up

Another use for a vibrator, particularly a smaller type such as the bullet or egg, is for her to hold it in place on her clitoris during intercourse.
I'm advised that doing so has the potential to produce "a real screamer" of an orgasm for her.

Chilly Con Carnal

Place the small, all-metal ben wa balls in the refrigerator (*not* the freezer!) at least an hour before sex, then insert them into your vagina just before he enters you. Actually, almost any metal toy — chains, cock rings, what-have-you — can be "chilled out" this way for an interesting sensation. A bowl of ice water kept by the bed can also be useful here.

Cheek to Cheek

Take his penis into your mouth, then apply a vibrator to your cheek. Move the vibrator sensously from one cheek to the other. Touch it to your lips. Apply it to the point of your chin. Turn your head so that the head of his penis makes a bulge in one of your cheeks and apply the vibrator to that bulge.

No Holes Barred

Another way that anal intercourse can be made more enjoyable for the woman is if a vibrator is used in her vagina at the same time. Try different sizes and types of vibrators, as well as inserting them either before or after she has been entered.

10

Stir Well and Serve

Instead of pressing the vibrator directly onto her
clitoris, try circling around it. Vary the speed with
which you make these circles, and the direction,
and the amount of pressure you're applying.

11

Magic Fingers

Insert two fingers into her vagina, then
twist and thrust them in various
pleasurable ways.
Now apply the vibrator to the base of
your fingers and repeat.

·12·

Not-Too-Hot Sex

Plug-in type vibrators often heat up during extended use. If your vibrator has been turned on for a while, touch the head – especially any metal parts – with the backs of your fingers to make sure that it hasn't gotten too hot to apply to your partner. (By the way, several Tricksters caution that the vibrators which have a heating element in them are nice for body massage but get dangerously hot for genital play.) Most plug-in vibrators are not built to be kept on for a long time, and will burn out if they're allowed to run too long. Smart Tricksters who enjoy extended play therefore keep *two* vibrators so they can trade off when things get a bit too warm.

·13·

It Keeps Coming, and Coming...

It is, of course, a very good idea to keep spare batteries on hand. An Urban Myth states that batteries last longer if kept in the refrigerator. Studies show this is not true to any substantial degree. What seems more important is that the batteries be kept dry – and the average refrigerator is a very humid environment. Storing your extra batteries in a cool, dry place, such as the floor of your bedroom closet, is a much better idea. Also, battery packages come with expiration dates, so it's easy to keep track of when replacement is needed.

14

It's a Hit

Hold the vibrator slightly above her vulva, turn it on, then lightly tap her there. Wait a few seconds, then repeat the tap. Increase, then decrease, the frequency of the taps. Increase, then decrease the forcefulness of the taps. Stay alert for feedback from your parner. The welcome degree of force can vary from mild and infrequent to heavy and frequent.

15

"Hey, Mabel, What's Wrong With the TV?"

Any device that converts electrical energy into mechanical energy, such as a drill, saw, refrigerator, or vibrator, can interfere with nearby radio or TV reception. This is particularly true if the TV and the vibrator are on the same electrical system – as they might be in a house or apartment building. To help cut down on any possible problems, go to a local electronic store and purchase an inexpensive AC line filter. Plug your vibrator into the filter and the filter into the wall socket. Another possible option is switching to a battery-operated or rechargeable vibrator.

16

Watch Your Legs

While using a vibrator is often a great source of pleasure, there are a few conditions that warrant caution. Be careful about using a vibrator if you have been diagnosed with phlebitis, or of using it on unexplained pain in your calf or thigh. You don't want to jiggle a blood clot loose that could travel to your lungs and cause a pulmonary embolism. Those can be as serious as a heart attack.
Also, be careful about using a vibrator on swollen or inflamed skin, particulary if you have some medical condition that causes decreased sensation in these areas.

17

Slip-N-Slide

Many lady Tricksters report that a vibrator feels too harsh on their clit or vulva without lubrication. Try applying a nice coat of water-based lube to one or both before you begin.

18

Drop & Mop

Ever had trouble at the end of a session remembering which toys need to be cleaned? A simple solution: When you're through using a toy, drop it on the floor. (If you're not sure whether you might want to use it again during the same session, spread a clean cloth or T-shirt on the floor where you're going to drop it.) At the end of the session, anything on the floor gets whisked away to the bathroom or kitchen for cleaning.

19

Keeping Time

Have her lie on her back, and sit between her legs with the base of the vibrator in your hand. Place your hand on the bed, then move the head of the vibrator in an arc from one of her thighs to the other, crossing over her vulva as you make the swing. You can vary the degree of pressure, the amount of time you take to make each arc, and the length of the arc. One sneaky "tease tactic" is to start by making very large, light, slow arcs and gradually make them smaller, heavier, and faster.

·20·

Stuff & Roast

If you enjoyed the Spanking Tricks in "Tricks 2," imagine
how much more you'd enjoy them with a butt plug in place!
The spanker may want to try landing a couple of smacks,
gently at first, right on the butt plug, to provide an extra
"jolt" of stimulation. (Watch out for the tailbone.)

·21·

Cool Vibes

Yes, it's yet another ice cube Trick.
In this one, stimulate her outer and inner labia with an ice
cube (try the cube against your moistened finger first to
make sure it's not so frozen that it will stick to her moist
tissue) as you apply a vibrator to her clitoris.

·22·

Two-Timing

If one vibrator is good for her, two may be
even better. Try putting one into her vagina and
applying a second to her clitoris.

·23·

The Magical Vibrating Weenie

Grab that vibe, guy, and hold it against the base of your cock while she performs fellatio on you. Why should she be the only one to have vibrator fun?

·24·

Coordination Challenge

While your partner is sitting on the bed or chair and you're kneeling at their feet performing oral sex, keep yourself entertained by using a vibrator on your own genitals. Careful — don't bite them when you come!

·25·

Fading In & Out

Slowly bring the vibrator close to their penis or vulva until it's just barely touching. Continue pressing until the pressure becomes very strong. Then slowly reduce the pressure until the vibrator has once again lost touch with their skin. ⦙ An alternative approach is to leave the vibrator off while you apply gradually increasing pressure. Once you get to the "medium" level, suddenly turn it on. Then slowly continue to increase the pressure. If the vibrator has different speeds, you can experiment with different pressure levels and different vibration settings.

26

By Yourself

One fundamental rule regarding sex toys that
you buy for yourself is to try them solo before trying them
with a partner. This is often true even if
you and your partner are very intimate and close. "Getting
to know" a sex toy is an extremely personal experience.
Things may go better if it's "just the two of you" for your
first few encounters.

27

A Vibrator Built for Two

Several Tricksters mentioned that if the woman uses a
(strong) vibrator on the front of her vulva, below her pubic
bone – sometimes called the external g-spot – during
doggy-style intercourse, he can feel the vibrations, too.
One lady mentioned, "This is a great, non-threatening way
to get him used to including the vibrator in mutual play,
because there's something in it for him too."

·28·
Butterfly Season

There are several different styles of butterfly-type vibrators on the market under various names. Basically, a butterfly is a shield-shaped vibrator made of soft latex or jelly-like material, usually with the power pack attached via a long cord. It comes with narrow elastic straps that go around her thighs and/or waist, holding it in place against her vulva. ǁ In addition to using the butterfly for self-play, some lady Tricksters like to wear theirs during doggy-style vaginal or anal intercourse. Some also enjoy wearing a butterfly during vaginal or anal intercourse while she lies on her back with her legs over his shoulders.

·29·
Up Against the Wall

In this slightly yoga-like Trick, she lies on her back on the floor, bending herself into a letter "L," with her bottom close to a wall. She lifts her legs up on the wall and uses the wall to brace a vibrator either inside her or resting on her clit. (Some folks feel that the legs-up position increases blood flow to the genital area, enhancing the sensations there.)

30.

Pat the Doggie

A lady who is getting happily spanked in a standing, bent-over or doggy-style position may express even more enthusiasm if she's allowed to use a vibrator on her clit during the spanking. (In fact, your hand or arm might wear out before her backside does.)

31.

Outlook Hot & Wet

Apply some "hot" lotion to his penis – the type that feels warmer when you blow on it. (Not Ben Gay or something similar.) Now put one or two ice cubes, or some crushed ice, in your mouth and fellate him.

33.

The Cheek Stretcher

Place a small, bullet-shaped vibrator in your cheek, then give him head. To reduce clean-up hassles, first drop the vibrator into an unrolled, unlubed condom, then tie a knot in the condom behind it.

·34·

G Whiz!

Many people call the g-spot the "female prostate."
Whether or not that's anatomically correct, it's functionally
correct when it comes to vibrators. The g-spot attachment
for a wand vibrator – a plastic cap, with a long crooked
"finger," that snaps on over the vibrator head to access
those hard-to-reach places – does a wonderful job
stimulating the male prostate. (Not sure which way to
insert it? If he's lying on his back, put it in so that the
"finger" is crooked upwards, toward his penis,
against the front wall of his rectum.
When you hit the prostate, his
reaction should be quite noticeable.)

·35·

A Cup of Silicon To Go, Please

Many coil vibrators come with a "cup" attachment
that's supposed to go over the head of a male cock. Most
men I've talked to don't get much out of this type of
vibration. However, the cup attachment does a
good job holding a properly sized silicon dildo – and silicon
transmits vibrations very well.

.36.

Deeper Throat

If you're having problems performing fellatio because of
your gag reflex, try applying a local anesthetic to suppress
it. Benzocaine, a good one, is found in a number of sore
throat lozenges and is one of the main ingredients in
Pleasure Balm. Apply some to the back of your throat,
wait ten to fifteen minutes, then enjoy.

.36.

Pearls Are So Versatile

Insert some brand-new or *extremely* clean anal
beads, or perhaps a string of pearls (make sure
the clasp stays outside), into her vagina. Then insert a
vibrator alongside them, turn it on, and enjoy.

.37.

Pearls Are So Versatile #2

Drape a string of pearls across her clitoris,
hold them firmly in place, and touch the vibrator to them.
Experiment with varying the sensation from mild
buzzing to vigorous bouncing.

·38·
Wonderful Wipes

Diaper wipes make excellent toy cleaners, particularly for the initial clean-up immediately after a session. They often contain alcohol and nonoxynol-9, so a quick swab of a toy with a diaper wipe right after the session is over can make the more "formal" cleaning up later on go easier.

·39·
An Interesting Speculation

Insert a vaginal speculum (inexpensive clear plastic ones are available in some erotic boutiques) and open it wide, then touch a vibrator to it. The sensations will be transmitted throughout the vaginal walls.

·40·
Press the Button

Many women enjoy having the vibrator pushed against their clitoris or pubic mound harder than you might imagine. Try slowly increasing the pressure and see how she reacts.

·41·
Bag of Tricks

If you're playing away from home, pack a few one-gallon zip-lock bags in with your sex toys. Any toy that needs cleaning goes into the bag so you can carry it home without dirtying your other toys. (Some sex party givers have started putting these bags out along with their other safer sex supplies for exactly this purpose.)

·42·
Playing Chopsticks

Combine a long, narrow, rigid implement such as a chopstick with a strong vibrator to vibrate into tiny little places, or to sharply localize the vibration to a larger place. Hold the chopstick loosely in one hand with its tip against the part you want to stimulate, then touch the vibrator to its base.

·43·
Wrist Twist

Many Tricksters swear by the so-called "Swedish" vibrators – the ones that attach to the back of the hand, thus turning your entire hand into a vibrator. However, some people find that fastening one of these toys to the back of the hand and using that hand for genital stimulation runs a risk of painfully pulling pubic hair. If you have this problem, try attaching the vibrator to your wrist instead.

44

Cubes & Balls

Put an ice cube (one with no sharp edges or corners) in your hand, and apply your hand to his well-lubricated penis. Now touch a vibrator to the base of his penis while you masturbate its head. (If you're using a plug-in vibrator, be *very* careful that no part of the vibrator except its plastic head gets wet.)

45

The Layered Look

You probably already know by now that using a toy first for anal play, then for vaginal play, is a great way to start a serious vaginal infection. Multifaceted Tricksters place two or even three condoms or gloves over a vibrator or dildo, then simply remove one barrier in order to move the toy from anus to vagina. (They find that the dildo doesn't mind the loss of sensation too much.)

46

The Waterproof Vibrator

Pull a condom entirely over a (battery-operated only, please!) vibrator and tie the end in a knot. You now have a vibrator that you can take into a hot tub, bathtub or shower.

47
Dunk-N-Doze

Hopping out of bed after great sex to go scrub and sanitize your toys is not most people's idea of fun. Some Tricksters keep a bowl or bucket of cleaning solution (see "How To Clean Toys After Use") by the bed and just drop their dunkable toys in to soak as they snooze blissfully. If you're using a bleach solution or some other strong-scented concoction, you may want to keep the receptacle covered or stow it in a nearby bathroom.

48
Rotary Sander

When inserting a dildo, vibrator, or similar hand-held object into your partner's rectum, keep in mind that twisting, spinning motions may be considerably more abrasive to the rectal lining than regular in-and-out motions. The more twisting you do, the less time your partner may be able to handle anal play —
no matter how much lubricant you use.

:49:

The Postman Rings Twice

There have been several incidents in which a man had great difficulty removing a metal cock ring once it was in place. Try using a rubber cock ring of the same, or perhaps even slightly smaller, circumference. If you can get that one on and off easily, you probably will have little trouble with the metal one.

:50:

Staying At the Y

Butt plugs (particularly those of smallish circumference) have the nasty habit, with only the slightest encouragement from a cough or contraction, of making rather dramatic projectile exits. Unless your scene involves "target practice," consider the following: acquire two strips of one-inch leather (as long as needed). Tie one around your partner's waist. Split the second one down the middle halfway so it forms a "Y" shape. Tie the unsplit end to the back so it acts as a thong/g-string nestling in the crack of the buttocks covering the anus, thus holding the plug in. The "Y" section can then part and go around either gender's genitals to be tied to the waist strap in front, leaving either pussy or cock free for further machinations.

·51·

Thuck Me, Baby!

Touch a small, battery-operated vibrator to the underside
of your tongue during oral sex, thus turning your tongue
into a vibrating sex toy.

·52·

Ring-A-Ding-Ding

Metal cock rings can set off metal detectors, as can ben wa
balls. Keep this fact in mind when traveling to airports,
courthouses, and other places where metal detectors are
in use – or you may find yourself having to make some very
embarrassing explanations.

·53·

What Could Ever Come Between Us?

When using a strap-on dildo, the rubber or
silicone base can be abrasive, or pull on the wearer's pubic
hair. A small piece of soft leather, cut to shape,
can be placed between the mons and the dildo
base to ease this friction a bit.

·54·

Neatness Counts

To dispose of your various safer sex supplies
after you're done playing, try this Trick. While still wearing
a glove, remove any condoms that need to be removed,
pick up any tissues, etc., and hold them in the palm of your
still-gloved hand. Now remove the glove by turning it
inside out. Tie a knot at the base, and everything will be
enclosed therein.

·55·

Leather and Rubber

All you leather-lovers out there probably
already know that insertable toys made of
leather, such as dildoes, can be very hard to
clean. It's therefore especially important that these
be covered with a condom before they're inserted (or
else kept for use on only one person and only one orifice,
and cleaned as best you can afterwards).

•••••
56
•••••
Backing Up

The initial entry of anal intercourse is often the most painful part for the receptive partner. This pain can often be minimized by holding the plug or dildo stationary and letting them "back" onto it at their own pace. Entry can also be made easier if the receptive person bears down (as they do when having a bowel movement) while the object is inserted. ⋀ Tricksters who enjoy using butt plugs on themselves often set the plug down, business end up, on a chair or toilet seat cover, and gradually lower themselves onto it. One "vertically challenged" lady I know finds the average chair too high for this maneuver, so she likes to place her plug between her bottom and the outside (external) corner of her shower stall, then back onto it.

•••••
57
•••••
Gone But Not Forgotten

Even if the battery in your phallus-shaped vibrator is completely dead, or the vibrating mechanism has given up the ghost, it can still give her hours of pleasure used as a dildo. (Many women report that their orgasms feel considerably more satisfying if there's something in their vagina when they come.) Simply inserting it and leaving it there while you masturbate her or perform cunnilingus can make a very pleasant difference.

58
When Push Comes to Shove

Take the tip of your vibrator and place it between their
genitals and their anus (the perineum). Turn it on,
and begin to press there. Build pressure until
it's almost painful, then slowly back off.

59
Give Her a Hand

Reach between her legs from above and place
your hand over her vulva, with her
clitoris at the bottom center of your
palm. Then touch the vibrator to the
back of your hand. Experiment with
different degrees of pressure and different
vibration settings. (This can be a good way to
cushion the sensation of a vibrator that feels too strong.)

60
Waste Is A Terrible Thing to Mind

Be careful where you dispose of your used condoms,
gloves, diaper wipes, tissues, etc. Small children and pets
may find such items, left in an open wastebasket, quite
inviting – and latex goods can be a strangulation risk as
well as a possible source of disease transmission.

·61·

Juggling Balls

Encircle the top of his scrotum with your thumb and forefinger. Squeeze this ring together until it's snug and his testicles are "trapped" below it, then slowly pull down until the skin of his scrotum is pulled tight over his testicles. Now, apply your vibrator to the tight-skinned sack. (Note: pulling down too quickly, too long, or too hard could cause damage; be sure to get feedback from him.)

·62·

Reduce the Richter

Sometimes even the lowest setting on a vibrator produces vibrations that feel too strong. If this happens, try wrapping a towel around its head.

·63·

Frothing at the Mouth

Take a sip of champagne or a soft drink, hold it in your mouth and insert his penis. (This maneuver itself can be very intense.) Now touch a vibrator to your cheek and notice his reaction.

64

Squeeze & Shake

Squeeze your genital muscles tightly, then apply the vibrator
to your genitals. Hold the squeeze for
three to five seconds, then release, and remove the
vibrator. Wait a few seconds, then repeat.

65

Heartfelt Sigh

Apply the vibrator to the "tender bit" of your
choice, then bring your mouth in close
and let your hot breath accompany the
vibration. Back away a foot or so and blow
a jet of cooler air onto the area. Go back in
close, lick the area to moisten it (if it's not
already wet), and repeat the process.

66

Wet & Wild

Soak a washcloth with warm-to-hot (not too hot!) water
and squeeze out the excess. Apply this cloth to the
genitals: wrap it around his penis or place it on her vulva.
Press a battery-operated vibrator to the cloth.

$\overset{\cdots}{\underset{\cdots}{67}}$

Seismic Mountain

The "Climb the Mountain" Trick described in "Tricks" and "Tricks 2" can also be done with a vibrator. It's a particularly useful Trick if you know that the recipient can reach orgasm from vibrator stimulation. Apply the vibrator for ten seconds, then remove it and caress the genitals sensously for ten seconds. Re-apply the vibrator, this time for eleven seconds, followed by ten seconds of sensuous caressing. Then apply it for twelve seconds, followed by ten seconds of sensous caressing. ⦙ This Trick, alternating ten seconds of sensual caressing with ever-lengthening periods of more arousing genital stimulation, can cause a very slow build-up to a very powerful orgasm.

$\overset{\cdots}{\underset{\cdots}{68}}$

Smooth Operator

Sharp edges on a dildo, vibrator, or butt plug do not bear thinking about – but manufacturers aren't always as careful as they should be, and there have been reports of cuts. Inspect a new sex toy carefully before you use it for the first time. Use sandpaper, a nail file, or an emery board to file down any sharp or rough areas.

:69:
The Lazy Daisy

This intercourse Trick offers a pleasant and relaxing way to integrate a vibrator into your sex play. In it, both partners lie spoon-like on their left sides and he enters her from the rear. She then twists her upper body so that she's lying on her back from the waist up, with his head at the twelve o'clock position and hers at about the two o'clock position. They then have intercourse while she uses a vibrator on herself. This position also allows eye contact at the moment of orgasm. This can be a good position for intercourse if the man is tired. It can also be a good position if one partner is heavier than the other or if one or both parties is full from having recently eaten a heavy meal.

:70:
Brrrrrrr!

One simple but very effective vibrator trick is to apply an ice cube to one of your partner's "tender bits" and then touch the head of the vibrator to it.

·71·
Soft Vibrations

Combine the touch of fur with the touch of a vibrator.
Lightly drape a piece of soft fur – or fake fur if you don't
like to use animal products – over the vibrator's head.

·72·
They Don't Make Band-Aids
Flexible Enough

There are occasional reports of injuries from the
use of a male sheath attached to a vibrator.
These sheaths sometimes have sharp or rough edges from
careless manufacturing, and the strength of the vibration
may mask the injury. A lady Trickster therefore
advises that you first check the interior carefully with your
fingers before inserting your cock. "This is a good rule of
thumb for any cavity," she quips.

·73·
One Jacket, Size Small

It's always wise to cover a butt plug with a condom before
inserting it. However, small plugs are difficult, if not
impossible, to adequately protect this way.
One elegant solution is to put the entire butt plug into a
condom and knot the end behind it.

:74:

No Fuzz Here

A wise lady Trickster advises against using ordinary towels to dry off toys that are used for insertion. She's had too many reports of lint becoming attached to the toy and causing problems the next time it's inserted. She advocates simply letting the toys air-dry instead. She also advises placing the toys on a T-shirt to dry instead of on a towel. Again, they're less likely to acquire lint that way.

:75:

Size Does Matter

A favorite general type of Trick is to have a vibrator in one orifice while his cock is in the other. I hear consistent reports that a smaller vibrator works better in the anus if the cock is in the vagina and a larger vibrator works better in the vagina if the cock is in the anus (particularly during doggy-style intercourse).

.76.
Dot's Right

One wise lady Trickster reduces the chances of acquiring an anal-to-vaginal infection by reserving some toys only for anal play and others only for vaginal play. (She does this even though she is quite diligent about cleaning her toys after using them.) She tells them apart by marking the ones used for anal play with a dot of red nail polish on a part of the toy that doesn't get inserted.

.77.
A Hole Separate Thing

This same Trickster also stores her anal toys and her vaginal toys in physically separate locations. That way, she reduces the chances that an anal toy will accidentally contaminate a vaginal toy by coming into physical contact with it.

.78.
If It's Empty, Fill It

Many of the attachments that come with vibrators, such as g-spot stimulators, are made of hollow plastic. A knowledgeable Trickster tells me that if you fill up the hollow places with silicon caulking compound, the toy will have a warmer, more lifelike feeling.

·79·

Hair You Are

Some Tricksters enjoy the "bristly" sensation
created by attaching a hairbrush to a vibrator. Be careful
this doesn't get so intense that it actually scratches the skin.
(This even feels good on your scalp!)

·80·

Wetter on the Dryer

For this trick, you'll need a dildo that has a
suction cup on its base, a clothes
dryer, some tennis shoes, and a few
towels. Attach the dildo to the top of
the dryer so that it's sticking straight up.
Toss the tennis shoes and the towels
(they can be wet if you like) into the dryer.
Then climb onto the dryer (be careful!), lubricate the
dildo as needed and slide yourself onto it. Turn on the
dryer and enjoy the ride. The tennis shoes will provide
"jolts" that will rock the dryer in a pleasant way
and the towels will muffle the sound somewhat.

:81:

Little Douche Coup

Several lady Tricksters report that they can decrease their odds of getting a yeast infection after a sex toy and/or lubricant session by douching soon afterwards. Preferred douching solutions vary: some recommend using a medicated douche, while others feel that a simple water and vinegar douche (a couple of tablespoons of vinegar in a standard-sized douche bag or bottle) is adequate.

:82:

Cleanliness Is Next To...

Feeling horny and grungy at the same time? Try attaching a suction cup dildo to your shower wall (be careful of slippery shower floors). "It's a great way to wake up in the morning, particularly if you've given up caffeine," says the Trickster who gave me this idea.

:83:

When You've Outgrown Your Rubber Ducky

Toy cleaning always seems like a bit of a chore to me, but one Trickster suggests an easy solution: when she showers off after play, she takes the dunkable toys that have been used on her into the shower to clean them.
(If you don't have a shower planned right away, toss the toys into the stall or tub to wait for you.)

84

Sticky Lips

Be careful about getting lipstick onto a
silicone dildo during dildo-sucking games,
or while putting a condom on one with your mouth.
The color can be very difficult to remove.

85

Patience Is a Virtue

If a woman says it hurts when you thrust a
dildo or vibrator (or a penis) into her,
it might mean that its tip is hitting her
cervix. Consider the following possible
remedy. ▯ Under normal circumstances,
her cervix may protrude into her
vaginal canal. However, when she becomes aroused,
muscles deep in her abdomen lift her cervix up and away
from the canal, and often even cause a slight hollow to
form at the end of the canal. ▯ Therefore, if
penetration hurts, try stimulating her clit until
she's more aroused, then try again.

·86·
Two, Two, Two Vibes in One

Put one vibrator into her vagina and another into her anus. (Don't switch them back and forth.) Alternate strokes with them, or move them in and out at the same time. Try turning them on one at a time, then both together. Vary the lengths of time each one is on. Combine this with masturbating her or performing oral sex on her.

·87·
Jelly for One

Latex or soft "jelly" dildoes can be very absorbent – soap, bleach, and other materials can be drawn in and be hard to remove – so consider carefully which cleaning solution to use. One Trickster recommends that such a toy be used *only* on one particular person, then cleaned with large amounts of warm running water *only* and allowed to air dry.

·88·
Give Her Some Lip

Grab her outer labia and pull, gently but firmly, down towards her feet. Hold both labia in one hand. Once they're pulled taut, apply the vibrator to her labia, or to your hand, or alternate between the two.

·89·

No-Expiration Date

Got a hot date tonight? Make "put fresh batteries in toys" part of your pre-date checklist. Battery failure at the height of passion can be sooooo disappointing.

·90·

Sweet Thang

Many women report that using sex toys increases the number of yeast infections they get. Sometimes the culprit is not the toy itself, but the accompanying lubricant. Many lubricants, particularly "flavored" lubricants, can cause infections if used internally. As the old saying goes: "Sugar grows yeast." Read the lubricant's label carefully. If it contains fructose or corn syrup, that may be what's causing the infection; avoid internal use. (Sorbitol usually causes no problems.)

91

Sweet Thang #2

Women who report an increased number of yeast infections following the use of a lubricant during vaginal sex might consider that the problem may be with the glycerin. If I read my medical books correctly, glycerin ($C_3O_3H_8$) is actually a sweet-tasting, syrupy, trihydric alcohol more properly called glycerol and widely used as a lubricant. Glycerol may also be a growth medium for yeast, so some women may benefit from using a lubricant that does not contain it. A British-made lubricant called Liquid Silk contains no glycerin and is gaining in popularity.

92

Surfin' USA

Ladies, try lying face down on your wand vibrator, with the shaft under your belly and the head against your pussy. You might enjoy moving your labia and clit with your fingers to bring different "tender bits" into contact with the vibration.

.93.
Ankle Yank

This Trick works well for solo or partner play. Insert well-lubricated anal beads one by one into the rectum. Pull one foot in close to the buttocks (this can work in face-up or face-down positions) and attach the ring at the end of the beads to a cord tied to the ankle or toe. During masturbation, you can straighten your leg to pull out the beads at the moment of orgasm. During partner play, the game is to turn your partner on so much that they stretch their legs in ecstasy, thus pulling the beads out for an extra thrill.

.94.
Shake & Bake

With a plug-in vibrator in one hand and a plug-in hair dryer in the other, you have some formidable potential at your disposal.
The combination of heat and vibration can be very powerful. Just be sure to get feedback from your partner. The heat could become unpleasant if continued too intensely for too long on any one particular spot.

·95·

Meet You In the Middle

Insert two fingers into her vagina, then press a vibrator
down onto her abdomen just above her pubic bone,
as though you were trying to push the vibrator down
toward your fingertips. If she enjoys g-spot sensation,
this may put her over the edge.

·96·

Hot Tip

Try attaching a q-tip to the head of your
vibrator to give an intense local sensation.
Dry q-tips, wet ones and ones made slippery
with oil or lube all feel a little different.

·97·

StairMaster

Insert a butt plug and/or a vibrator, then walk
up and down the stairs. (Stay near the banister.
You may need to grab it.)

·98·

Fingers First

While many people like to be anally penetrated by
someone wearing a strap-on dildo, it may not be
smart to rush directly into this activity.
A wise woman who has played this game with many
different partners advises first inserting some gloved
fingers. Feel for any unusual bumps, roughness, or swelling,
and watch for any blood. If the recipient can take two
fingers, then try using a hand-held dildo on them.
If that goes well, *then* you can try moving
on to the strap-on type.

·99·

Brush 'Em Brush 'Em
Brush 'Em

Attach a toothbrush to the vibrator. You'll probably
need two rubber bands, spaced at least an inch apart.
Try the "electric toothbrush" on her clit or his
dickhead, or on either of their nipples, or other
"tender bits," for an interesting reaction.
Careful not to let this get *too* intense.

100

Too Darn Hot

Prolonged exposure to low heat, or exposure to high levels of heat, can damage condoms, latex gloves, and sex toys. Keep this in mind when deciding where to store your toys. Don't place them too near a heating duct, radiator, or similar heat source.

101

Don't Finish Your Finish

Think twice before placing any lubricated item on a varnished surface (such as a wooden table or chair or a hardwood floor). The lubricant may dissolve the finish.

102

Bend & Stretch

Tricksters new to anal play can "train" themselves to accommodate a plug (or a penis). Insert a plug (see Trick 56 for self-insertion ideas) and leave it in for a while, until you hardly notice it's there any more. Then try easing it in and out a few times (add more lube if you need it). Many Tricksters find that they can take a larger plug if they insert it themselves than they can if someone else does it.

103

Which Vibrator Is for You?

The wide variety of vibrators out there can be confusing. If you're buying a plug-in vibrator, your basic choice is between the wand-type vibrators (shaped like a shaft with a larger head) and the coil-type ones (shaped like a hairbrush with a shaft onto which attachments can be placed). If you're a woman, one possible hint is to notice how you use your fingers when you masturbate. Do you use a wide, side-to-side motion or do you use a more focused up-and-down motion? If you're a side-to-side kind of gal, try the wand. Up-and-downers may prefer the coil.

104

Shake 'Em Up, Baby

Ladies, you may change your mind about those ben wa balls lying abandoned in your nightstand if you try inserting them before using a vibrator on your clit and vulva.

105

BYOV

If you're playing with someone who has their own
vibrator, use it — not your vibrator — on them.
This is not just good safer-sex practice; many people are
used to their own vibrator and have an easier time getting
off with it than with an unfamiliar kind.

106

Get a Leg Up

Position can matter a great deal when using sex toys,
especially regarding masturbation. Some Tricksters
report that the position of their legs is particularly
important: they can reach orgasm with their legs in one
position, but not in others. They use this to good effect
when they want to prolong (or shorten) their session.

107

I Want a Man With a Slow...

This can be a good Trick if the man has problems with
premature ejaculation. (It also can work quite nicely for
couples having no problems.) Basically, the man thrusts in
and out of the woman *very slowly* while she uses a
vibrator on herself. This may help the man to last
longer and the woman to come.

108

Vibes for Guys

Vibrators aren't just "girl stuff," fellas. Try using a vibrator on various parts of your genitals – many male Tricksters enjoy the vibration on their penis (particularly on the underside just below the head), their perineum, and the outside of their asshole. If it's her vibrator you're using, or if you want to use it on someone else later, cover it carefully with a condom, rubber glove or plastic wrap, or put plastic wrap over the part of you you're stimulating.

109

Everything In Its Place

While many women enjoy insertion play with a standard vibrator, it was not specifically designed for vaginal insertion. Many report better results by first inserting their favorite dildo, then touching a strong vibrator to the dildo's base.

110

Numb and Number

Many women, and some men, report that lengthy use of a vibrator on their genitals causes the area to "numb out" to an annoying degree. Here is a relative scale of "numb out" activities. ⫯ A. Pulling back the clitoral hood and applying the vibrator directly to the clit produces the fastest "numb out." ⫯ B. Applying the vibrator through the clitoral hood is slower than A. ⫯ C. Applying the vibrator to the labia is slower than B. ⫯ D. Applying the vibrator to the labia through a light piece of cloth (such as the corner of a handy sheet) is slower than C. ⫯ E. Applying the vibrator after its head has been wrapped in a heavy towel is slower than D.

111

Flrrrrrrrrttt...

One flirtatious lady Trickster likes to put a small vibrator in her purse and take it along on a first date, then arrange for it to "accidentally" go off. "I love seeing the expression on his face when he realizes what he's hearing," she says.

112

Slow In Slow Out

Be sure to remove your anal toy slowly and carefully.
Yanking it out feels unpleasant and could cause injury.

113

They're the Expert

While it may be fun to use your partner's vibrator on them,
please don't feel too bad if they have trouble reaching
 orgasm from your ministrations. Many people
can only reach orgasm if they use
their vibrator themselves. So, when
that time comes, hand it over.

114

Feeling Thick

Many women report that shorter, thicker vibrators,
dildoes, and so forth feel better in their vaginas than the
longer, more slender, ones feel. More than a few also
prefer a dildo that has a curve to it.

115

Towel Off

Wrap the vibrator in a towel, put it between your legs
against your genitals, and squeeze your legs together for a
long count. Relax for a while, then repeat.

116

Jacket Required for Entrance

While bullet and egg vibrators are not recommended
for anal play – it's too easy to yank the cord loose when
you try to withdraw them – some Tricksters first
place the vibrator in the end of a fully unrolled condom and
then insert it, leaving the base of the condom outside the
rectum to aid in removal. The Reality female condom, with
its inner ring (the one at the closed
end) removed, also works well for this Trick.

117

Who Needs to Be Naked?

A strong vibrator can be excellent for
"real" quickies. You don't even have to
undress, just apply it through your clothing.
As one lady Trickster reported to me,
"It will even go through a snowsuit."

118

Mmmffphth...

Hold the base of the dildo in your mouth
and fuck your partner's mouth with it.

119

Evening Ensemble

Going out for the evening? He can wear his
leather cock ring in the usual way and she can wear an
identical one on her wrist. Nobody but the two
of you will know that you're a "matched set."

120

Whirly Bird

Place a large dildo in a strap-on harness and
practice pelvic thrusts. When you
can do "helicopters" you are really
working your pelvic muscles – toning and
trimming for good sex. (Richard Simmons,
eat your heart out.)

121

Who Gloves Ya, Baby?

A condom is a tight fit over the head of a large wand
vibrator, but a glove goes on easily. If you like,
you can wrap and tie a couple of the fingers together
under the head of the vibrator to hold the glove on more
firmly. ▯ If you enjoy a g-spot stimulator with your
vibrator, the thumb of a latex glove stretches easily and
neatly over the "finger" part of the attachment.

122

It's All In the Timing

Many Tricksters enjoy anal play but are grossed out by small amounts of fecal matter on (animate or inanimate) toys. Right after a bowel movement may be a good time to do anal penetration play. If that timing isn't convenient, you may want to try a ready-made drugstore enema about half an hour to an hour before you play.

123

Batteries Not Included

One large adult toy distributor notes that many toys that get returned as "defective" actually just have the batteries put in the wrong way. If batteries in a toy are side-by-side, they should be going in opposite directions. If they're same-end to same-end, they should all be going in the same direction. Also, always remove the batteries from your toys if they're not going to be used for a while (more than a week or so).

124

A Warm Feeling Inside

Applying cold lubricants to sensitive body parts can be momentarily uncomfortable. Many Tricksters recommend placing the bottle of lubricant in some comfortably warm water for several minutes beforehand. (This Trick can also be used on toys that are safe to submerge in water.)

125

When You're Full, Take a Walk

Sex toys don't have to stay at home!
Many Tricksters enjoy the secretive, mischievous
feeling of wearing a dildo or butt plug out in public.
(You should probably avoid doing complex tasks such as
driving a car while you have it in you.)

Latex Allergy

As if we didn't have enough problems, it now appears that far more people are allergic to latex than was previously believed. In a recent paper presented by Dr. Dennis Ownby to the American Academy of Allergy and Immunology, 6.5% of all blood samples at a Red Cross blood bank tested positive for latex allergens. Furthermore, there have been several reports of allergic reactions so strong that they caused the person's death. The FDA has traced at least 16 deaths to severe allergic reactions to latex.

People who are sensitive to latex condoms can try the new Avanti polyurethane condom. (it's worth keeping in mind that such people may not be allergic to the latex, but to the lubricant applied to the latex. Try using a unlubed brand and notice if there is any difference.)

People allergic to latex gloves can try vinyl gloves. Again, some people turn out to be allergic not to the latex itself, but to the powder that sometimes coats latex gloves. Try powderless gloves.

Allergic reactions may dramatically increase in severity from one exposure to the next, particularly if the exposures occur several weeks (or longer) apart.

For very mild, localized allergic reactions, treatment with an anti-inflammatory or antihistamine cream might be all that's required. Creams containing hydrocortisone (anti-inflammatory creams) or diphenhydramine ("poison ivy" creams) will probably work well. Note that neither of these will treat an infection or directly relieve pain. To treat infection, use an antibiotic cream such as

Neosporin or Betadine. To treat pain, use a cream that contains lidocaine or benzocaine. Some creams contain both an antibiotic and an anesthetic.

For moderate reactions, which might involve localized itching, swelling, and inflammation, you might need to take an oral antihistamine in addition to a cream. Diphenhydramine is usually the drug of choice. It's sold under various trade names, including Benadryl and Sominex. I prefer the "sleeping pill" diphenhydramine tablets because they release the drug rapidly into your system. The initial dose of diphenhydramine for adults is 50 mg. by mouth..

For severe reactions, which may involve difficulty in breathing, urgent measures are necessary. Have someone call 911 immediately – this person needs to go to the hospital as quickly as possible.

A drug which specifically counteracts breathing difficulty can be purchased without prescription in almost any drugstore or supermarket. It's called epinephrine (adrenalin) and it's the active ingredient in over-the-counter asthma inhalers.

To use the inhaler, have the patient breathe in the medication, hold their breath for about fifteen seconds, then resume breathing normally. This procedure may need to be repeated a few times. If so, let the patient breathe normally for at least one minute between doses. The patient should not need more than three or four doses, particularly if an ambulance will arrive quickly. Also give them some diphenhydramine tablets. (Give them very little to drink – only enough to get the pills down.)

Diphenhydramine and epinephrine are the two major drugs used in the immediate treatment of severe allergic reactions. They are inexpensive, legal, and widely available. I recommend that you have them with you whenever you're in a situation where someone might have an allergic reaction and medical help is more than just a few minutes away.

Medical/political note: It's possible to purchase, if you have a prescription for it, a self-injecting syringe of epinephrine called an "Epi-pen" or "Ana-Kit." From what I've been able to learn, this costs more and works slower than an epinephrine inhaler, yet I've heard physicians discourage the use of non-prescription inhalers for reasons that sounded more political than medical to me. If you have a serious allergy problem, I'd certainly recommend that you consult a physician regarding the advisability of getting an Epi-pen, but that's something that I'd carry *in addition to* my epinephrine inhaler and diphenhydramine tablets.

If you or your partner has trouble with allergies, spend time down at your local drugstore or supermarket carefully reading the labels and accompanying information on the various creams, tablets, and inhalers. Notice which creams are good for inflammation, itching, infection control and pain relief. (No one cream is good for all four.)

If you know that you have serious allergies, it's crucial to consult a knowledgeable physician. They may be able to administer therapy that will de-sensitize you. Also, diphenhydramine and epinephrine do not mix well with certain other medications – particularly some anti-depressants – and your physician can tell you more about that.

Unfortunately, we are living in a time when more and more people are developing more and more allergies. People with allergies will benefit greatly by learning as much as they can about how allergic reactions develop and what they can do to help manage them. This knowledge can literally be life-saving.

How to Clean Toys After Use

Attempting to "sterilize" a toy is usually neither necessary nor practical. You can, however, remove or kill so many micro-organisms that there aren't enough to transmit a disease. (The saying that "it only takes one" is just simply not true. It usually takes several million.) In other words, you can reduce their number below an "infectious concentration" and make it difficult or impossible for them to multiply.

Bugs are just like us in many ways. They need water, protection from extremes of heat and cold, something to eat, shielding from toxins, and a means of reproducing. If any of these gets disrupted too badly, soon the bugs won't exist any more.

Imagine that your favorite sex toy is lying over there on the ground with numerous nasty bugs on it. How might you clean it?

First of all, ask yourself a few questions. They'll determine what approach you take.

Who will this item be used on in the future? If it will only to used on the same person, decontamination isn't such a major issue. (If it's been in her rectum, or if she has a yeast or other vaginal infection, cleaning is difficult, so use a condom on the toy to help prevent further contamination.)

If it will be used on others, it will need a *much* more thorough cleaning. Let's assume it's something you can get wet. First turn on some gently running water. Then put on latex (or other nonporous) gloves, pick up the item, and place it under the stream of water. Be sure no splashing occurs. Let the water run over it for a few minutes. Don't rush. What you're going for here is the physical removal of the bugs. Turn the item until all surfaces are thoroughly exposed.

If the item is absorbent, such as a "jelly" or latex item, and you know that it's only going to be used on the person it was previously used on, you might stop here. Absorbent toys can retain various cleaning agents which can cause irritation or other problems later. Place the item on a low-lint cloth, or other place where it won't pick up any foreign bodies, and allow it to dry.

If the item is nonabsorbent, such as a plastic, silicone, or metal item, rinse it, scrub it with soap for a few minutes, then rinse again. (Simply placing the toy in the top rack of the dishwasher can be an excellent way to accomplish the entire cleaning process.) Don't underestimate the value of this step. A thorough washing with soap and water can remove up to 97% of all bugs.

Soap note: Certain types of soaps kill bugs better than others. In particular, nonscented, liquid soaps containing triclosan (such as "Dial" liquid soap or a generic equivalent) are highly recommended.

Plug-in vibrators and battery-operated vibrators can be wiped with an cloth moistened with bleach solution or alcohol. If you use bleach, a "follow-up" wiping with water or alcohol will be needed to remove any bleach residue. Be sure not to get the "innards" wet.

If you believe that the item needs a more thorough decontamination, you can soak it in a number of cleaning solutions. Remember this principle: *soak for a minimum of twenty minutes.*

Nonabsorbent items can be washed, then soaked in a solution made from nine parts water to one part 5.25% sodium hypochlorite bleach (common household bleach) for at least 20 minutes. This is a very powerful disinfectant with a very broad spectrum. *It is the preferred cleaning agent.* Be sure to use a bleach-water solution that's not more than a few hours old. Rinse with water or alcohol to remove any bleach residue. After rinsing, set it aside to dry.

Nonabsorbent, and some absorbent, items can be soaked for at least 20 minutes in a solution containing at least 60% ethanol or isopropyl alcohol. Alcohol evaporates rapidly, so it may be wise to use a covered container. Note that alcohol is not as broad spectrum a decontaminant as bleach and water.

Metal objects can be boiled for at least twenty minutes. Obviously, other items can't tolerate this degree of exposure to heat.

Leather items such as whips can be very difficult to clean. Wipe them down with soapy water, then wipe them again with alcohol (bleach is more likely to decolorize), and set them aside to dry. They may need to be re-oiled afterwards.

A quiet note about handwashing: more frequent handwashing can do a lot to decrease the spread of infectious disease. (It dramatically reduces the spread of the common cold, for example.) The protective value of washing your hands after you play, and after you clean your toys, is not yet fully appreciated.

Cleaning toys can be something of a chore at first, but with time it becomes "just another part of it." Also, the time spent cleaning your toys can be a delicious time to contemplate how, when, and on whom they'll next be used.

What to Do If You "Lose" Something In the Rectum

Most "formal" anal toys have a wide flange at their base to prevent their being pulled all the way in. Items without a flange, such as ben wa balls, cordless vibrators, and so forth, are not recommended for anal play. Use dildoes that lack a widening at the base only if you can keep a firm grip (with your entire hand, not just a few fingers) on them at all times. Note that the large amount of lubricant required by anal play can make keeping such a grip a definite challenge.

Every now and then, something "vanishes" into the rectum – particularly if it's something not specifically designed for anal play. This vanishing act can happen if a curved part of the rectosigmoid colon suddenly "unbends" a bit or if the item goes in beyond the sphincters.

If this does happen, keep in mind that the item will almost undoubtedly pass back out naturally and on its own before long. The natural peristaltic action of the bowel will prevent the item from working its way farther up. There's no need to mount a dramatic rescue operation. Above all, *don't do anything that hurts*. The item should appear no later than the next bowel movement. Assuming a squatting position, as opposed to the usual sitting position, may help pass the object.

(Caution: mild to moderate bearing down is probably OK. Hard straining could damage the rectal passage – and, particularly if the individual has a heart condition, could possibly slow the heartbeat or even precipitate a cardiac arrest.)

You might be able to reach the item with a fingertip. If so, you may be able to ease it down until you can grasp it and (gently, slowly) extract it. One major caution: be careful not to push the item farther in. Sitting or standing in a upright position, or walking around for a while, may help the item work its way back down to where you can reach it.

Inserting an ounce or two of additional lubricant into the rectum may also help. At this point, a more liquid lubricant (such as mineral oil) is probably better. Careful use of an enema bulb or turkey baster can help ensure that the lubricant goes into the rectum. The individual should lie on their left side as the lubricant is inserted, and for several minutes thereafter, then sit, stand, or walk.

A few don'ts:

1. No enemas, please (other than as mentioned above). Large volumes of water are not what the intestine needs just now. Among other things, the water may push the object further in, where it can *really* get stuck.

2. No stimulant or irritant-type laxatives such as senna, bisacodyl, or castor oil.

A few possible options:

1. Simply waiting is a very rational strategy. There is a good chance that the item will pass out naturally. (If it isn't passed with the next bowel movement, the odds of your having to seek medical aid greatly increase.)

2. Eating a meal can trigger the gastro-colic reflex and thus cause a bowel movement approximately 30 to 60 minutes afterwards, as can drinking a caffeine-containing

beverage – perhaps especially a warm, caffeine-containing beverage.

A few warning signs:

1. The person has a prior history of rectal, anal, or other bowel problems. (You *did* check this before you started stuffing things up there, didn't you?)

2. The person develops cramping abdominal pain, other bothersome abdominal pain, fever, or blood starts coming from their rectum. If any of these appear, it's time to see a physician immediately.

3. The object hasn't passed on its own after twenty-four hours. Again, it's now time to see a doc.

Subpoint: If this could happen to you, think for a moment about where you'd go. This may not be something you want on your regular, permanent medical record. A visit to a local free clinic, women's clinic, or other resource may be more appropriate. Your local erotic boutique or SM-oriented leather store may be able to give you the name of a discreet, sex-positive physician. If you have a sex-positive, discreet friend who is a physician, nurse, paramedic, chiropractor, or other type of medical person, you may be able to get advice and/or a referral from them. Also, a sympathetic physician may be found by contacting local sexuality-related organizations such as clubs for gay men, lesbians, bisexuals, transgender people, or SM folks. You may not have to give your real name, but please be open regarding medical information – and pay your bill if at all possible.

It is very wise to have your "plan B" doctor lined up ahead of time. Trying to find such a person while under the stress of an urgent situation can be very difficult. Some stores and clubs keep listings of "friendly" health care professionals. Sexuality author and educator Race Bannon maintains a list of physicians, chiropractors, therapists and other professionals who offer sexually nonjudgmental services; to receive a copy, send a self-addressed business-sized envelope with two regular stamps on it to Kink-Aware Professionals c/o Race Bannon, 584 Castro St. #518, San Francisco, CA 94114-2500, or e-mail him at 72114.2327@compuserve.com.

Summary

By far the best way to deal with this situation is to not get into it in the first place. Careful selection and use of toys for anal play will prevent most problems. If something does get lost, remember the odds are that it will find its own way back without too much help from you.

The Five "Shuns" of Anal Play

The anal region has a good supply of nerve endings. Skillfull anal play can be very rewarding, both physically and psychologically. Reports of orgasm from anal play alone are not rare. Still, this is not something that one should rush into.

The anus and rectum are not "intended" for insertion. While fingers, butt plugs, dildoes, vibrators, anal beads, and other items have all been inserted successfully, this area of erotic play requires a high level of awareness.

The various issues of successful anal play can be looked at in terms of the five "tions" (shuns). They are, in the approximate order you'll need them: information, protection, lubrication, relaxation, and communication.

Information

The receptive person should tell their partner about their past experiences (or lack thereof) regarding anal sex, particularly any problems that have occurred. They should also mention any anal or rectal problems they have, such as hemorrhoids, fissures, an enlarged prostate, or more serious medical conditions. (People with heart disease should know that heavy bearing down, during anal play or during a bowel movement, can slow the rate and force of their heartbeat, sometimes to zero. Use appropriate caution and seek medical consultation as necessary.)

Protection

Disease can be transmitted in both directions during anal play. For this reason, barrier usage is very strongly recommended. Dildoes, plugs, vibrators and penises should be covered with condoms. Hands and fingers should be covered with gloves. Toys and hands should be cleaned afterwards.

Lubrication

The vagina and the mouth supply their own lubrication; the rectum does not. While the vagina sometimes needs a little extra lubrication, the rectum *always* does. In general, "heavier," more gel-like lubricants tend to work better than the "lighter," more liquid-like lubricants. Nowadays, water-soluble lubricants are preferred over oil-soluble lubricants, particularly if latex condoms and/or gloves are being used. Colored or scented lubricants should probably be avoided. Remember: "Lube early; lube often."

Relaxation

While erotic fiction contains many depictions of a person having something shoved suddenly and deeply into their rectum by an uncaring, dominant partner, the reality is far different.

The anus has two rings of sphincter muscle: the external and the internal. The internal takes longer to relax. Start very gently and ease in only one finger. (Placing a cotton ball in the fingertip of your glove can help eliminate any "sharp" feeling.) Use lots of lube, don't move the finger around too much, and pay close attention. You may actually feel the sphincter relax. When you can move one finger in and out easily, add more lube and try slowly inserting a second finger. I recommend you not insert a vibrator or dildo until you can easily thrust two fingers all the way in and out. Having this done to you will teach you a great deal about how to do it to someone else.

Communication

Successful anal penetration requires feedback. Even a small variation in pressure, location, depth, or angle can make a major difference in how well the play goes. The "receiving" partner must communicate these matters clearly and promptly to the "giving" person so necessary adjustments can be made. Above all, the receiving partner shouldn't "tough it out" in silence in order to please their lover. If something feels wrong, it almost undoubtedly is wrong and needs prompt correction. Failure to take corrective action can put the receptive person in the hospital. There are even reports of fatalities. Anal play is *not* the time for the receptive partner to take a "stoic heroic" approach. Ongoing communication and adjustment are essential.

So there are the five "tions" of anal play. One useful way to remember them is to remember that there is one for each finger. Can you name them "off the top of your hand"?

Twenty SM Safety Tricks

I consider SM the riskiest form of sex. It has all the risks associated with "vanilla" sexuality, plus the very real physical, emotional, and relationship risks that go along whenever one person binds, dominates, or "tortures" another.

I have written a comprehensive guidebook to this very rewarding and very risky form of sexuality. It's called "SM 101: A Realistic Introduction" and there's a good chance it's available from the same place that you got this book. All of the matters listed below are discussed in far greater depth and detail in that book. If SM is becoming a serious interest of yours, please consult "SM 101" for more information. There is also a great deal of useful information in the "Spanking Tricks" section of "Tricks 2: Another 125 Ways To Make Good Sex Better."

I have very strong reservations about "quickie" SM instruction, but I have to face the fact that most of the stores that sell this book also sell SM gear such as restraints, blindfolds, gags, clamps, paddles, and whips and such devices are, after all, most definitely sex toys. I'm therefore going to include some basic SM safety precautions in this book. This information is *not* meant to be adequate instruction. Rather, its purpose is to steer you away from the most common, major hazards.

By all means, check out some of the SM books recommended herein. If you can, contact a local SM club for additional instruction. Also, you can find some first-rate educational material regarding SM on the Internet. Check out the newsgroups alt.sex.bondage, alt.sex.femdom, and alt.sex.spanking, and use the various World Wide Web search engines to discover the many excellent resources available there.

SM Safety Tricks

1. Be very careful about who you let tie you up.

You might think that this would be so obvious as to not be worth mentioning. I have found differently. Bondage need not be dangerous in and of itself, but it most definitely is dangerous in terms of the vulnerability it creates. When two people are alone together, that's one degree of risk. However, when two people are alone together and one of them is tied up, the degree of risk dramatically increases. Be very wary of someone who "only" wants to tie you up. You are quite literally trusting them with your life.

I strongly recommend that you let someone tie you up only after you have first done at least two SM-type sessions with them that didn't involve any bondage. While all SM encounters have some risk attached, the first few SM sessions you do with a new partner are by far the ones most likely to "go wrong."

Subpoint: Limit the amount of bondage during the first few times you try it. My general rule is that the first time I let someone tie me (after a few successful non-bondage sessions), I'll only let them tie my hands to each other. I will let them tie my hands behind my back, but I most definitely will *not* let them tie me to something such as a bed or chair. I won't let them tie my elbows, my knees, or my ankles in any way. I also won't allow them to blindfold or gag me the first few times we play together. (Among other things, they're going to need the feedback provided by my voice and facial expressions.)

A common suggestion is "Let's try some bondage. I'll tie your wrists and ankles to the four corners of the bed. It won't hurt." You can see how this involves way too much vulnerability for a first-time session.

2. **Experience it yourself, preferably several times, before you do it to someone else.**

The more empathy you have with what the other person is experiencing, the better partner you'll be and the more the both of you will benefit. There's an adage in the SM community that it's better to start out in the "submissive" or "bottom" role. This is true *if* you have access to an experienced, empathetic, ethical partner (lucky you!) and *if* you can assume such a role without too much emotional difficulty. If either is not true, then maybe you're better off not doing that — at least for a while. It is entirely possible and valid to start off in the "dominant" or "top" role.

If doing a "submissive internship" (which can vary widely in its length, intensity, and variety) isn't an option, do what you can to experience what they're experiencing. Try applying that toy to your own body. Try kneeling on the floor yourself for a while. Try staying in the position you want them to remain in while bound. (Be careful about tying yourself up. See later in this book.) The more empathy you have for what the submissive is experiencing, the better dominant you'll be.

3. **Play with a "Silent Alarm" in place.**

When I play privately with a new partner, I always have what's called a "silent alarm" in place. What that means is that somebody I trust knows where I am, who I'm with, and what we're doing. If I fail to check in with this person by a certain time and in a certain way, they will know that I'm in serious trouble and things will start to happen — sometimes up to and including calling the cops. (I'm very serious about this. I have called the cops myself when someone I'm "baby sitting" has failed to check in.)

The primary purpose of a Silent Alarm is *deterrence*, not after-the-fact arrest of the perpetrator. Therefore, I always let my new partner know ahead of time, as diplomatically as possible, that such a device will be in place while we're playing. Furthermore, I urge them to do the same.

A good partner will understand and not be upset or angry about my using a silent alarm. Furthermore, they will *not* question me regarding details of how the alarm is set up. Any show of negative emotion on their part, or any questioning regarding how my alarm works or why I felt the need for it, are major red flags that I should just simply not play with this person, ever. If they are new to the practices of SM, I might politely advise them *one time* that such questions are considered out of line. If they still continue, it's time for me to forget the whole thing.

4. Use only plain paraffin candles for hot wax play.

Many people are now aware that it's possible for one person to drip wax from a burning candle onto their lover's skin as a from of erotic play. One major word of advice: use *only* plain white paraffin candles. Colored candles, and candles made of materials such as beeswax, may melt at a much higher temperature. People have suffered third degree burns from having such candles used on them. Also, be sure to drip a few drops of that wax onto your own skin (the back of your hand works well) before dropping it onto your lover's skin. Notice how the temperature of the wax varies according to the height from which it's dropped.

5. Avoid leather toys with sharp edges or corners.

While the equipment sold in "formal" SM stores tends to be of excellent quality, the equipment sold in other stores may not be. In particular, when considering purchasing something made out of leather such as a whip, a collar, or a set of cuffs, check out their edges and corners. A quality piece of equipment will have these places rounded off and smooth to the touch. A shoddy piece of equipment may have amazingly sharp edges and corners. You can imagine how human skin will react to being whacked by something so sharp. If you find such a piece of equipment, tell the store manager that you're not buying it, and tell them why.

6. Don't whip someone over their kidneys (or liver, or spleen).

While almost any place on the body except the eyes and ear canals can be struck *very* lightly, heavier blows must be confined to the more padded areas. The head, neck, arms, and lower legs (including the knees) are basically just not suitable as targets for a whip. In particular, avoid heavy blows to the abdominal cavity. Place your hands on the crests of your hips. Now place them on the bottom of your breastbone at the notch where your ribs come together (the xiphoid process). You'll want to stay below the hip crests and above the xiphoid process.

The best area on the back for whipping is lower half of the upper half. The best area on the buttocks is the lower half. (The inner, lower quadrant is frequently the most erotic place, and is known in SM circles as the "sweet spot.") As always, experience and feedback are essential.

7.   Clamps hurt most when coming off.

When a clamp is applied to a nipple or to some other tender body part, it compresses the tissue and blood is forced from the area. (This means that the area now has no blood supply. Experts differ regarding how long a clamp should therefore be left on, but their answers are all expressed in terms of minutes, not hours.) When the clamp is removed, blood rushes back into the tissue and re-expands it – and that hurts!

There is nothing that can be done to prevent this pain. It can help somewhat to remember that the acute phase will only last for a period of several seconds (milder residual soreness may last longer), to develop a skilful hand when it comes to removing them, and to remove one clamp at a time, with the submissive signaling when they are ready to have the next clamp removed.

It's wise to experiment with ordinary, inexpensive, spring-type, wooden clothespins before buying more "formal" clamps. While people can vary widely in how they react to having clamps applied to them, as a rule the more experience you have with applying them to, leaving them on, and removing them from your own body the better you'll become regarding using clamps on someone else's body.

8.   Keep it friendly.

Do SM only with people you know well, and are on good terms with, and when you're both in a good mood. Playing SM with a stranger, with someone you're not on good terms with, or when one or both of you is tired, upset, intoxicated, or otherwise not at your best, dramatically increases the degree of risk.

9.   Watch out for their tailbone.

A heavy blow to a person's tailbone (coccyx) can cause a very painful sprain, dislocation, or even fracture of that part of their body. This can be particularly true if they are bent over at the waist. The size, apparent position, and angle of the tailbone can vary quite a bit from person to person. Before giving them a spanking or whipping, take a moment to feel their tailbone. Also, if you move them from a "straightened out" to a "bent over" position, take a moment to feel if it's now more prominent.

10.   Negotiate what you'll do ahead of time.

As I say in "SM 101": "When two people are alone together, and one of them is naked and tied up, and the other is standing over them with their hands full of torture implements, this is *not* the time to have a serious mismatch of expectations." Adult-to-adult negotiation before playing is standard practice among experienced SM practitioners. Indeed, many SM folks pride themselves on their non-manipulative, highly ethical, negotiation skills. (Negotiation is dealt with at great length in "SM 101." There's even a negotiation checklist.)

Negotiations can cover the types and duration, of bondage, what sexual acts will and won't occur, what types of spanking or whipping will or won't occur, and many other matters. Experienced SM people can often conduct a full negotiation in five to ten minutes. Less experienced people may take hours. That's fine. It's far better to do more negotiating than you need to than less negotiating than you need to.

Important subpoint: During the SM play, it's important to stick to the limits set by the pre-play negotiation. It's particularly important that going further than previously agreed not be proposed during the play by the dominant partner.

11.   Check in with each other afterwards.

In order to properly deal with the SM session, the people involved need to spend "straight time" (out of role and in a non-sexual context) discussing what happened and their reactions to it. There are three basic check-in times:

Immediately afterwards. No major discussion is usually needed or advisable here. Just a brief reassurance that both parties are basically emotionally and physically OK.

The next day. By now, the participants have had a chance to intellectually and emotionally react to the play. This is the best time for a "debrief" regarding what happened to discuss thoughts and feelings, what worked and what didn't, and so forth. It's also usually the soonest time to discuss if and when the two people involved will play again.

About a week later. This is the time to deal with any emotional "aftershocks" that may have come up. It's also a time to deal with any physical problems that may have not been apparent immediately afterwards or the next day. (Both of these occurrences are rare, but they do happen.)

12.   Bondage Safety Tip #1: Loss of sensation.

There is never any need to tie any body part so tightly that it loses feeling. If some part of your lover's body "goes to sleep," then it's time to loosen whatever's causing the problem.

13.   Bondage Safety Tip #2: Quick release.

If you tie someone up, you must have some method of releasing them quickly. That means you must be able to get them completely free within sixty seconds, and preferably within thirty seconds.

One basic safety precaution is to keep a pair of scissors handy so you can cut your lover free in an emergency like a fire or earthquake. The large, plastic-handled "paramedic scissors" popular with rescue squads are an excellent choice because, unlike regular bandage scissors, they were designed to cut through leather, webbing, and other heavy materials quickly. These scissors are available at many medical supply stores. The more health-conscious and responsible leather stores and erotic boutiques also carry them.

Both nylon stockings and silk scarves – often the first choice of beginners – are notoriously difficult to untie if the knots have been pulled really tight. Don't use anything you're not willing to cut through if necessary.

14. Bondage Safety Tip #3: Stay with them.

Many people think it would be fun to "tie them up and then go off and leave them." In fact, this is one of the most dangerous, irresponsible things you can do. It's a crime in many areas. Furthermore, if your partner is injured in any way while you are gone, even if they asked you to leave them, you could face major criminal charges.

Here's a simple rule: Always stay as close to a bound person, and check on them as often, as you would an infant left in your care. If you gag them, stay even closer and check even more often.

15. Bondage Safety Tip #4: Emergency lighting.

A bound person needs to be closely watched. In an emergency, they need to be immediately freed. To do both of these in an efficient manner, you need light. A power failure during a normal sexual encounter can be, at the least, annoying. A power failure during a bondage session can be a serious, even life-threatening, problem.

Therefore, responsible bondage fans always make sure they have emergency light sources immediately available. Flashlights, especially light-colored ones that are easy to see, are carried in pockets, stored in specific places in "toy bags," and otherwise placed where they can be easily found in the dark.

Furthermore, increasing numbers of bedrooms and "playrooms" now have "blackout lights" – lights that come on automatically if the power fails – plugged into their wall sockets. Basic models that will do quite nicely for the average-sized room can be bought at drugstores, variety stores, and similar places for around ten to twenty dollars.

16. Bondage Safety Tip #5: The dangers of self-bondage.

Many people have bondage fantasies but no partner, so they bind themselves. The person interested in self-bondage faces a problem. They want to bind themselves so they can't escape, yet, obviously, eventually they will want release. What to do?

Self-bondage can be extremely dangerous. You know how risky it is to bind someone and then leave them alone. The self-bound person has this obvious problem.

I have heard of several deaths resulting from self-bondage that went wrong. Even more disturbing, many of these deaths involved highly experienced players who "knew what they were doing" yet died anyway. Most such fatalities involved gags, hoods, ropes around the neck, or some other devices that had the potential to restrict breathing.

Most self-bondage involves locking devices, especially around the wrists. The person works out some mechanism by which the keys again come within their grasp. If the device fails to work (and, sooner or later, it *will* fail) the bound person often has no other way to get free or summon help.

Also of critical importance, bondage not tight enough to put the bound area to sleep quickly may still be tight enough to do that gradually. The self-bound person's hands may go numb after an hour. If the keys fall within reach after that – trouble.

I experimented for a while with self-bondage, but gave it up after I had an incident that gave me a moment of nearly pure panic. I also found that, besides its dangers, self-bondage has other drawbacks.

First, you may rapidly discover that being in bondage without a "sweet tormentor" for company is *boring*. The vibrators, clamps, dildoes, and other gear that aroused you when you first put yourself in bondage may feel awful after your arousal fades – even if it doesn't malfunction or go out of adjustment. If, genius that you are, you set the situation up so you can't get loose for three hours, you may find that the last two hours and fifty minutes go on for a *very* long time.

You might try binding your breasts and genitals, but be very conservative about using anything that would restrict your breathing (gags, hoods, neck ropes), make you vulnerable to a fall (blindfolds), or restrict your limbs – especially your arms.

Self-bondage often seems like a good idea in fantasy, and offers plausible exploration, as long as *absolutely nothing* goes wrong. Remember that even a minor maladjustment of a piece of equipment can set the stage for hours of genuine suffering, and that a serious malfunction or unexpected development can cause you to die a slow, agonizing death. Many "experts" died exactly this way.

17. "One to ten."

Raise your hand about twelve inches above the receiver's buttocks and let it drop. Tell the receiver that the stroke they just received had a strength of three. A "two" is about half that forceful, and a "one" is little more than a very light touch. The strength of the spanks can go all the way up to "ten" with each spank above three being about 25% stronger than the previous number.

Tell the receiver that when they call out a number, it will indicate both the strength of the spank they are willing to receive *and* that they are willing to receive it. Tell the receiver that this number can *both* increase and decrease.

This Trick is very useful in helping the receiver, particularly a novice, retain their emotional balance. They are thus much more likely to open up to and enjoy the experience.

18. Keep "reality" out of it.

Spanking fans often role-play situations (naughty pupil and teacher, disobedient child and baby sitter, etc.) to act out spanking fantasies. These scenarios often involve someone getting "punished" for some supposed "misconduct." All well and good.

However, it's *very* important to keep real world situations out of spanking games. Spanking someone because they forgot to pay the phone bill, left the lights on, or did something similar that you really didn't like, can be a recipe for disaster. Spanking games are consensual, erotic, fantasy play, not a place to settle scores or grudges. Those get handled in "straight time," not in the bedroom.

19. Harder is not necessarily better.

People who enjoy giving and/or receiving spankings vary tremendously in how hard they want their spankings to be, and how often they want to give or receive one. It's important for each individual to find out what works best specifically for them. Just remember: Harder is not necessarily better. More painful is not necessarily better. Longer is not necessarily better. More often is not necessarily better.

20. Two squeezes means I'm OK.

A spanking can create its own intense world for the receiver. Sometimes the giver will want to check on the receiver's well-being without asking a direct verbal question – doing so could spoil the mood, also receivers sometimes "go under" into a deep, non-verbal part of themselves.

A very effective alternative to checking in verbally is for the giver to take the receiver's hand in theirs and give it two firm and noticeable, but not painful, squeezes. Each squeeze should last about one second and there should be about a one-second pause in between them. This is understood to ask the question, "Are you *basically* OK with what's going on here?" The receiver signals back that they are (at least) basically OK with the situation by giving the hand of the spanker two squeezes in return. (It is, of course, essential that you and your partner get clear on this point *before* the spanking actually begins.)

If the spanker squeezes the receiver's hand and gets no reply, they should wait about ten seconds and then repeat the two squeezes. If another ten seconds brings no "reply squeezes," it's time to make verbal contact.

Problems

Probably the most important advice I can give you regarding finding help for the problems listed below, and other problems, is to grab your phone book and start looking. Many communities have local resources. Check the first few pages and look over the table of contents. Look up these and related topics in both the white and yellow pages. Check your phone book for an index.

If this doesn't help much, go to your local library and look through the phone books of nearby communities, particularly those of nearby big cities.

Local newspapers and magazines, particular free or low-cost ones that come out on a weekly or less frequent basis, often carry valuable listings. Gay and lesbian papers can be particularly helpful. Look them over carefully.

The Internet is an excellent source of information regarding sexuality-related problems. Look in the alt.recovery, alt.sex and alt.support hierarchies, in any newsgroups that announce local events and groups in your community, and on the World Wide Web.

Abuse/Battering/Neglect

National Domestic Violence Hotline (800) 799-7233

National Child Abuse Hotline (800) 422-4453

Parents Anonymous (800) 249-5506

AIDS

National AIDS Hotline (800) 342-AIDS

National STD Hotline (800) 227-8922

Birth Control/Abortion

Check your local yellow pages under "Birth Control Information Centers." Note: Some anti-abortion agencies have been accused of being less than totally honest about that fact. If a given resource doesn't explicitly say that it offers abortions, please consider that its policies may be anti-abortion.

Censorship

American Civil Liberties Union
132 West 43rd St.
New York, New York 10036
(212) 705-7496

National Coalition Against Censorship
132 West 43rd. Street
New York, New York 10036
(212) 807-6222

People for the American Way
2000 M. Street N.W., Suite 400
Washington, DC 20036
(202) 467-4999

Death During Sex

People, especially older men, die during sex far more often than is commonly believed. One of the reasons for this is that their partners are often too embarrassed to tell what was going on when the death occurred.

Studies have shown that the person in the community who faces the highest risk of sudden cardiac arrest is a man over the age of 50, and the person most likely to be with him when it happens is his wife. If your boyfriend or husband is over 50, I strongly recommend that you both take a CPR class.

Studies have also shown that the second highest risk group for a sudden cardiopulmonary emergency is, to simplify matters, anyone wearing diapers. If you help take care of young children, schedule a class that teaches infant and child CPR. (The technique differs considerably from that used on adults.)

You can look in the yellow pages under "First Aid Instruction" to find out where classes are offered. The American Red Cross, American Heart Association, some hospitals and emergency service agencies, and private firms all offer classes.

If you take a CPR class, try hard to get a good instructor. I suggest someone who has a minimum of one year of full-time experience in pre-hospital emergency care. A paramedic might be a good first choice. (Although people who are good at providing emergency care are not necessarily good at teaching others how to do that.)

Disabilities

The Lawrence Research Group, which publishes the Xandria Collection catalogs, puts out a specialized catalog of sex toys and advice for people with disabilities. This catalog also contains a page listing of sexuality resources for the disabled across the U.S. To receive this catalog, send $4 and a request for the Special Edition for Disabled People to:

Lawrence Research Group
P.O. Box 319005
San Francisco, CA 94131

Herpes

Herpes Resource Center (HRC)
P.O. Box 13827
Research Triangle Park, North Carolina 27709

These folks offer wonderful information for those coping with any aspect of herpes. Among other things, they sponsor a nationwide network of support groups. If somebody I cared about had herpes, I would make certain that they were fully informed about what these folks offer.

National STD Hotline (800) 227-8922

Incest

Incest Survivors Anonymous
P.O. Box 5613
Long Beach, CA 90805-0613
(310) 428-5599

Survivors of Incest Anonymous
P.O. Box 21817
Baltimore, Maryland 21222
(410) 282-3400

Both of these groups sponsor meetings all over the country. They will also help you start a group in your area if one does not already exist. Incest is one of the most under-reported forms of abuse in this country.

Old Age

Sex Over Forty Newsletter
PHE, Inc.
P.O. Box 1600
Chapel Hill, North Carolina 27515

As people age, their needs and their bodies change. This newsletter is one of the most informative and useful sources of information on the topic.

Rape

As soon as you safely can, call 911, a rape treatment center, or a similar resource. Check your phone book under Rape, Battering, and Sexual Abuse Aid. It's very important from a medical, emotional, and legal point of view to seek help as soon as possible after the assault. Know that an attempted rape can be almost as damaging, and take as long to recover from, as a completed rape.

If you can safely do so, have the authorities come to the scene so they can look for valuable evidence. Try not to shower, douche, brush your teeth, or change clothes until you've been examined.

If you need support or don't feel your case is being handled properly, by all means contact a rape crisis center for more help.

Sex Therapy

You don't necessarily need a formally trained sex therapist to help you cope with sexual problems. Many therapists with broader training do excellent work in this field.

That said, I want to mention that the organizations listed below help train and set policies for sex therapists. Someone representing themselves as a sex therapist would probably have extensive contact with at least one of them.

Sex therapy is not an exact science. In particular, such issues as the use of surrogates are highly controversial. You should understand that the organizations listed below are far from in total agreement on every issue. AASECT is considered the more conservative.

Society for the Scientific Study of Sex (SSSS)
P.O. Box 208
Mount Vernon, Iowa, 52314

American Association of Sex Educators, Counselors, and Therapists (AASECT)
435 Michigan Ave, Suite 1717
Chicago, Illinois 60611

Sex and Love Addiction

These are 12-step groups designed to help people achieve "sexual sobriety" by using the principles of Alcoholics Anonymous. They have chapters in many parts of the country. If one doesn't exist in your area, they will help you start one. (Don't be surprised if your initial outreach efforts draw more people than you expected.)

Sexaholics Anonymous
P.O. Box 300
Simi Valley, CA 93062

Sex and Love Addicts Anonymous
P.O. Box 119
New Town Branch
Boston MA 02258

Suicidal/Homicidal Feelings

Almost every local community has telephone crisis hotlines. Again, check your telephone book – particularly the first few pages.

Additional Resource Information

San Francisco Sex Information, at (415) 989-7374, offers referrals and a sympathetic ear. They most definitely do not, however, offer phone sex.

Alternative Sexuality Resources

As with the "Problems" section, many resources can be found by carefully checking in your phone book and by visiting the library to check the phone books of nearby cities, particularly large ones. Also, many alternative sexuality clubs and other resources advertise in adult papers and other periodicals with an erotic slant.

The internet is also an excellent source of information regarding most forms of alternative sexuality. The majority of sexuality newsgroups fall under the alt.sex hierarchy, but some, typically more oriented toward philosophy, politics and discussion, can also be found in other hierarchies such as soc.*. The World Wide Web also includes a huge number of pages with information, articles, photographs and resource lists on various alternative sexualities.

Important Notice: When writing to any of these organizations, it's wise to include a business-sized, self-addressed, stamped envelope.

Bisexuality

Bisexual Resource Center
Robyn Ochs
P.O. Box 639
Cambridge, MA 02140
(617) 424-9595

Body Size and Weight

National Organization to Advance Fat Acceptance (NAAFA)
P.O. Box 188630
Sacramento, CA 95818

A national support organization, with chapters in many cities, for fat people and their admirers.

Circumcision

NOCIRC (an anti-circumcision organization)
P.O. Box 2512
San Anselmo, CA 94960

Corsetry

For people who enjoy wearing corsets and people who enjoy people who enjoy wearing corsets.

B.R. Creations
P.O. Box 4201
Mountain View, CA 94040
Ask about their "Corset Newsletter."

Cross Dressing

ETVC
P.O. Box 426486
San Francisco, CA 94142
This is a respected educational and social organization for people exploring gender issues and those who care about them. It publishes a newsletter that contains many local resources, national resources, and information on other local groups around the country. Highly recommended.

International Foundation for Gender Education (I.F.G.E.)
P.O. Box 367
Wayland, MA 01778
(617) 894-8340
The organization publishes the "TV/TS Tapestry Journal," a 150+ page magazine containing articles, references and other resources. Sample copy $12.00. Again, highly recommended.

Expanded Families

PEP
Box 6306
Ocean View, Hawaii 96704-6306
   Nationwide organization promoting polyfidelity, group marriage, and expanded families.

Gay and Lesbian Resources

National Gay Yellow Pages ($10.00)
Box 292
Village Station
New York, New York 10014
   Again, your local phone book should help you find resources in your area.

Infantilism

Diaper Pail Friends
38 Miller Avenue #127
Mill Valley, CA 94941
   This is *not* about adults having sex with children. DPF is an organization for adults who enjoy dressing up and pretending to be babies.

Piercing, Scarification, and Other Body Modification
   The following magazines contain wonderful introductory information and referrals for those who are into having more than their nose pierced. Warning: Piercing, scarification, branding, and other forms of body modification can cause injury or death if done improperly. Proper training and supervision is essential; never attempt these practices without it.

Body Play and Modern Primitives Quarterly
P.O. Box 421668
San Francisco, CA 94142-1668 Sample issue: $12.00

Piercing Fans International Quarterly (PFIQ)
Gauntlet
8720 Santa Monica Blvd.
Los Angeles, CA 90069   Sample issue: $10.00

Pleasure Parties

In-home parties can be a fun, safe and comfortable way to order sex toys, lotions, lingerie and other accessories. Check your local phone book under "Lingerie – Retail" or "Party Planners." A large national provider is:

Coming Attractions Parties, Inc.
200 Valley Drive #10
Brisbane, CA 94005
800-4-PASSION

Prostitute Support Groups

(Mailing addresses only. For sex workers – no would-be customers need write!)

Coyote
2269 Chestnut Street # 452
San Francisco, CA 94123

Coyote – Los Angeles
1626 N. Wilcox Ave. # 580
Hollywood, CA 90028

Prostitutes of New York (PONY)
25 West 45th St., # 1401
New York, New York 10036

Hooking is Real Employment (HIRE)
P.O. Box 89386
Atlanta, GA   39359

Prostitutes Anonymous
11225 Magnolia Blvd. # 181
North Hollywood, CA 91601
 For those who want to leave the sex industry or for help afterwards.

Swinging

 This form of sexuality used to be called "wife-swapping."

North American Swing Club Association (NASCA)
P.O. Box 7128
Buena Park, CA 90622
 Publishes "International Directory of Swing Clubs and Publications."

Sadomasochism

 The following organizations are some of the largest. They are open to both men and women. They can provide referrals to those seeking all-male or all-female groups and to those seeking clubs closer to where they live. (Several new clubs form each year.)

Chicagoland Discussion Group
P.O. Box 25009
Chicago, Illinois 60625

Eulenspiegel Society (Believed to be the oldest SM club in the U.S.)
P.O. Box 2783 GCS
New York, New York 10163

Society of Janus
P.O. Box 426794
San Francisco, CA 94142-6794

Threshold
2554 Lincoln Blvd., # 381
Marina Del Rey, CA 90291

Tantra

Tantra, The Magazine
P.O. Box 79
Torreon, New Mexico 87061-9900

Tantra, and its cousins Quodoushka and Healing Tao, are spiritual pathways whose teachings and practices include sexuality. *Tantra, The Magazine* contains excellent listings and descriptions of classes, workshops, and other activities offered around the country.

Transgenderism

For those wishing to change their genders.

FTM (stands for Female-to-Male)
5337 College Ave. # 142
Oakland, CA 94618

San Francisco Gender Information
P.O. Box 423602
San Francisco, CA 94142

Gender Identity Center Newsletter
3715 West 32nd Ave.
Denver, CO 80211

TV/TS Tapestry Journal
Internatonal Foundation for Gender Education (IFGE)
P.O. Box 367
Wayland, MA 01778

Additional Alternative Sexuality Information

San Francisco Sex Information, at (415) 989-7374, offers referrals and a sympathetic ear. They most definitely do not, however, offer phone sex.

Bibliography

"A New View of a Woman's Body" by The Federation of Feminist
Women's Health Centers
published by Feminist Press
8235 Santa Monica Blvd., Suite 201
West Hollywood, CA 90046

"The Complete Guide to Safer Sex"
Institute for Advanced Study of Human Sexuality
1525 Franklin Street
San Francisco, CA 94109

"For Play: 150 Sex Games for Couples"
by Walter Shelburne, Ph.D.
Waterfall Press
5337 College Avenue, #139
Oakland, CA 94618

Condom Educator's Guide, Version Two
by Daniel Bao and Beowulf Thorne
Condom Resource Center
P.O. Box 30564
Oakland, CA 94604
(510) 891-0455

"Sex: A User's Manual"
by The Diagram Group

"Anal Pleasure and Health: A Guide for Men and Women" (Second Edition)
by Jack Morin, Ph.D.
Yes Press
938 Howard Street
San Francisco, CA 94103

"The New Our Bodies, Ourselves: A Book By and For Women"
by The Boston Women's Health Book Collective
A Touchstone Book
published by Simon and Schuster

"The Good Vibrations Guide to Sex"
by Cathy Winks and Anne Semans
published by Cleis Press

"The Black Book"
edited by Bill Brent
P.O. Box 31155
San Francisco, CA   94131-0155
A comprehensive national guide to sexuality clubs, stores, publications and other resources.

Please Send Me Your Tricks
(but read this carefully first)

Do you do something that consistently drives your lovers wild? Would you like to share your Trick with the rest of us? Send it to me! I plan to publish more "Tricks" books. Maybe you can be a contributor.

Send me your Trick, preferably typed on one side of a standard sheet of paper. Please date the paper and include illustrations as necessary. If I use your Trick, I'll send you a free copy of the book it appears in and, if you wish, put your name on the "thank you" list in that book. Because of "independent discovery" it's impossible for me to credit a particular person with a particular Trick. (I repeatedly encountered independent discovery while researching this book.)

Also, again because of independent discovery, I'll undoubtedly receive letters from different people describing essentially the same Trick, and I can only afford to reward the first person who clearly describes the Trick in question. So, again, please date your letter. (Actually, I'll probably send a book to the first three or so people who send in a given Trick.)

You can increase your chances of inclusion by sending more than one Trick. One per page, please. Please don't send more than ten Tricks a year. I wouldn't have time to properly consider them.

Let me know what type of credit you want on the "thank you" list. You may choose between anonymous, first name only, initials only, your nickname, or your full legal name. If you wish, I can also include your city. If you sign your Trick with your full name, be honest about your identity and include your address and phone number. Signing another person's name to a letter is a crime, and I will verify all full names before publishing them.

Please send your Trick only by regular first class mail. Spare me from certified letters, registered letters, and so forth. If you don't feel you can trust me, please don't send me your Trick. Also, please don't put a copyright notice on it. A unique usage of words can be copyrighted, but not what such words describe. (This is what allows dozens of reporters to each write a story about the same incident.) Also, I'd almost undoubtedly need to re-write your words while preserving the essence of your Trick.

Please don't send anything "too far out" or dangerous. Letters dealing with children or animals will be immediately turned over to the police.

Please don't send anything regarding political issues, economic concerns, social problems, and so forth. Again, those matters deserve books of their own. (However, if you know of a widely available resource that can help someone with a personal problem closely related to sexuality, I would love to share that information with my readers.)

I was utterly unprepared for the volume of mail that resulted from the publication of my other books. This will add to my load, and I'm already chronically behind in answering that. I therefore can't promise you an individual reply. Including a self-addressed, stamped envelope will help somewhat, but please don't get your hopes up too far. Also, I won't know until just before publication whether or not your Trick was included, so please don't write and ask. You'll know very shortly after I know.

I apologize if the above seems negative and restrictive, but it reflects learning from experience. If you would be happy with a book and being on the "thank you" list, but wouldn't be too disappointed if your Trick didn't make it, then I would genuinely love to hear from you. This world can use a little more pleasure. I hope you help contribute to that.

Send your Tricks to: Jay Wiseman, c/o Greenery Press, 3739 Balboa Ave. #195, San Francisco, CA 94121.

Other Books from Greenery Press

Bitch Goddess: The Spiritual Path of the Dominant Woman
ed. Pat Califia & Drew Campbell — $15.95

The Bottoming Book: Or, How To Get Terrible Things Done To You By Wonderful People
Dossie Easton & Catherine A. Liszt, illustrated by Fish — $11.95

Bottom Lines: Poems of Warmth and Impact
H. Andrew Swinburne, illustrated by Donna Barr — $9.95

The Compleat Spanker
Lady Green — $11.95

The Ethical Slut: A Guide to Infinite Sexual Possibilities
Dossie Easton & Catherine A. Liszt — $15.95

A Hand in the Bush: The Fine Art of Vaginal Fisting
Deborah Addington — $11.95

KinkyCrafts: 99 Do-It-Yourself S/M Toys for the Kinky Handyperson
ed. Lady Green with Jaymes Easton — $15.95

Miss Abernathy's Concise Slave Training Manual
Christina Abernathy — $11.95

The Sexually Dominant Woman: A Workbook for Nervous Beginners
Lady Green — $11.95

SM 101: A Realistic Introduction - 2nd Edition
Jay Wiseman — $24.95

Supermarket Tricks: More than 125 Ways to Improvise Good Sex
Jay Wiseman — $11.95

Training With Miss Abernathy: A Workbook for Erotic Slaves and Their Owners
Christina Abernathy — $11.95

Tricks: More than 125 Ways to Make Good Sex Better
Jay Wiseman — $11.95

Tricks 2: Another 125 Ways to Make Good Sex Better
Jay Wiseman — $11.95

Coming in 1998

Juice: Electricity for Pleasure and Pain, "Uncle Abdul"

Blood Bound: Guidance for the Responsible Vampire, Deborah Addington & Vincent Dior

Please include $3 for first book and $1 each for each additional book with your order to cover shipping and handling costs. VISA/MC accepted. Order from:

 greenery press

3739 Balboa Ave. #195, San Francisco, CA 94121
toll-free 888/944-4434   http://www.bigrock.com/~greenery